A Wish And A Prayer

Marisa Meyer

Published by Trellis Publishing, 2021.

This is a work of fiction. Similarities to real people, places, or events are entirely coincidental.

A WISH AND A PRAYER

First edition. July 2, 2021.

ISBN: 979-8224582303

Written by Marisa Meyer.

A WISH AND A PRAYER

MARISA MEYER

Nicola had given up all hope to find true love. After a disastrous relationship, she resigned herself to the fact that she was not meant to find love, but when her best friend's wedding draws near she has to come to terms with the fact that she would have to face the man who broke her heart, and smile and wave. Her friend Angelique makes her toss coins into the Trivia fountain and she does, only to please her friend, but little did she know what would unfold.

Kyle, like Nicola, had given up on love. In his opinion, some people find love and others are destined to go without it. He sees her from across the fountain, and he too makes a wish more to humour himself, but when an old man appears next to him and tells him that he has a week to make his dreams come true, strange things start to happen.

When legend and reality meets face to face, who knows what may happen next...

Chapter 1

Nicola spent the entire day sightseeing, trying to find what was left of the beauty that this place once held. She had spent most of her childhood here in Rome, went to school, fell in love, and fell out of love. Then she traveled the world only to come back to this so called magical place full of romance and wonder. The last few years, she had jumped from one relationship to the next, but they never lasted and her last relationship had been nothing short of a colossal disaster. After dating Carlos for almost a year, he ran off with one of the waitresses that worked for him and that had been the last straw. Now two years later, she was still single, still miserable and while all her friends had settled down around her, she had a bad case of once-bitten-twice-shy syndrome.

"Nicola, the right man will come around one day and when he does, he will sweep your feet out from under you," her friend Angelique said.

"Honestly, I don't want my feet swept out from under me. It leaves me fragile and injured every time," she mumbled and crossed one leg over the other where she sat at the small table at the Alfredo Bistro.

Angelique was due to be married in a few weeks, and she had asked her to be the maid of honor, which would be okay if the circumstances were different. What troubled her, was that the best man was Carlos, and chances were that his latest girlfriend would cling to his arm like a piece of gum to hair. Two years since he dumped her for some blonde hair bimbo, and she still seethed because he had her believe there was such a thing as true love. He treated her like a queen, promised her the world, and then wham, just like that ripped the carpet out from under her.

"Fine then, but you really do not have to feel bad for not having a partner, people go to weddings alone all the time," her friend said and waved the waiter over.

"I don't care about going on my own, I just don't want to be in the same room as Carlos, as simple as that," she muttered and dug in her purse for her wallet, "The last thing I need is for him to shove his new girlfriend in my face."

Angelique sighed and reached for her hand, "It's a few hours, and besides, I've set you two far apart so you won't have to even talk to him."

"And what about the opening dance?" Nicola asked with a raised brow.

"Well, it's one dance, and it will be over before you know it."

"I refuse to dance with him Angelique, if you insist, you'll just have to find a new maid of honor," Nicola said determinedly.

Her friend gasped with mock horror and fanned herself, "You wouldn't dare do that to me, would you?"

"Don't tempt me," she muttered, "I'm not dancing with him, he can dance with his girlfriend and I'll sit that one out."

"Fine then, you can sit it out, but I will find you a date, whether you like it or not."

Nicola laughed and shook her head, "You have enough on your plate as it is, no need to bother with my woes and disappointments."

The two friends paid for their meal and left the Bistro, they discussed the last few details of the wedding reception, gossiped about the guests Angelique's mom insisted on inviting. Angelique told her about Roberto's sister who is in total rebellion, all because her father refuses that she invite her UK friend to visit and attend the wedding with her. It was drama in paradise for most. But Angelique was her usual self, happy-go-lucky, with no care in the world.

"I think you should make a wish," Angelique said as they walked past the Trevi Fountain.

"Been there, done that," Nicola dismissed and carried on walking.

"Oh come one, just for fun, I'll also make one."

Nicola rolled her eyes and dropped her head, "You're impossible Angelique," she said and took the coin Angelique held out to her.

"So we close our eyes, make a wish and toss in the coin," her friend said excitedly.

Nicola did just that, and although she feigned boredom and irritability she silently made her wish and threw the coin as far into the fountain as she could. She had little hope and hardly believed in wishing upon stars, much less fountains.

"Done, can we go now?"

"Here you are!"

It was Angelique's fiance who caught up with them, and jokingly he wrapped his arm around Nicola's shoulder.

"Don't tell me that my dear fiance is up to her old tricks," he said laughingly.

Nicola smiled and playfully wrapped her arm around his waist, "She is indeed, she's insisting I wish upon a water drop."

Angelique waved her hand dismissively in the air, "You never know when dreams might just come true, just look how lucky I got."

Nicola laughed and looked up at Raoul, "I still cannot believe you asked Carlos to be your best man," she mumbled.

"Mi dispiace, but you know he is my best friend," he chuckled, "I may not agree with his choices in life, but we've been friends since childhood."

"I guess," she said and offered him a smile before stepping away from him, "At least you did not follow in his footsteps."

"Never!"

Chapter 2

I'm worried about you, the voice on the other end whispered sleepily.

"I'll be fine, I'm in Rome and having the time of my life sis," Kyle said as he paced up and down with his phone stuck to his ear.

His sister had always been overly protective of him, ever since they were kids. After his mom and dad were killed in the horror car crash that claimed sixteen lives when he was only ten, Alissa had taken him in; she was much older than him by then and fought tooth and nail to keep him out of foster care. She had given up everything to keep him with her. Thankfully her boyfriend, then, had offered to marry her just so that they could provide a stable home for him. Now almost twenty-four years later she is still happily married to Gary, they have their own two kids, who are like his own siblings and here he is, still single. Time after time, just when he thought he had met the right woman things turned out to be the opposite. His last love interest was a lovely girl, but she was a psychologist, and she kept picking at his brain as if he was a troubled bipolar individual. It all started off well, but then every time he grew quiet, she wanted to analyze his mood. It simply didn't work out and when he finally had enough, and told her it was over, she nearly came undone. A year later, she's married and picking on someone else's brain.

"I'll be back in a week or so, I promise," he mumbled as he glanced up at the majestic fountain.

As long as you keep in touch, I don't mind how long you take to come home.

He dug in his pocket and took out a coin and flicked it into the fountain, "Who knows, maybe I meet the love of my life here and never come home," he joked.

Now you're pushing it, Ella and Mark will miss you, so you better make sure you get home.

"Love you sis," he said and smiled as he killed the call.

He sat down on one of the benches that surrounded the fountain and stared blankly at his phone before looking up at the Trevi Fountain. Wishing wells had been around for centuries, yet they never really made any wishes come true. They were like falling stars making empty promises. He narrowed his gaze to the plaque against the side of the fountain and read the inscription.

For romance, with your back to fountain, place two coins in your right hand and toss it over your left shoulder into the fountain.

He smirked and shook his head, its absolute madness to thing that such a trivial thing can make any difference. He didn't believe in fate or destiny, much less wishing wells and stars.

While he sat quietly, taking in the serene beauty of his surroundings he spotted two women approaching the fountain. The one was clearly a tourist, with long blonde silk hair, while the other one looked like she belonged here in Rome. She had dark bouncy curls that framed her flawless face. She had an understated beauty but her smile did not reach her eyes. As he watched them he had to smile, they too were at the fountain making silly wishes. The girl with the curls turned her back on the fountain and just like the instruction on the plaque she tossed her coin into the water. Whether it was one or two he wasn't quite sure, but he was certain that she wasn't here looking for love. And when the tall man with the long brown shoulder length hair appeared and wrapped his arm around her, it confirmed his suspicions.

He watched them banter and when they had left, he stepped up to the fountain and turned his back to it, "Here goes nothing," he said and tossed the two coins he had over his shoulder.

At least it may someday feed a hungry child, he thought as he glanced into the water at the thousands of coins that lay at the bottom. Surely people have helped themselves to other's wishes. If this fountain was in New York, it would be empty by now.

"You have a week to find her," a disembodied voice spoke out of the shadows next to the fountain.

Kyle spun around to see who it was. And elderly man leaning on a cane stepped into the light. Wrinkles like lay lines mapped his face, and told their own stories, but it where the lines next to his narrow eyes that depicted a time of happiness and joy, maybe even love.

"Excuse me?" Kyle said as he studied the old man.

"A week, you made a wish at the same time she did," he said in his croaky voice.

"Who?" Kyle asked confusedly.

"The girl, she made a wish too."

Kyle frowned and looked at the fountain then back at the man but he was gone. He spun around and walked into the shadows but there was no sign of him. Confused he scratched the back of his head and then muttered, "Foolish dreams of old people."

The only girl here, who did make a wish, was the brunette he saw earlier, and she was taken, so the old man was clearly confused. He doesn't recall the blond tossing any coins into the fountain either and he was a hundred percent sure that there were no other people at the fountain. Why am I even entertaining this, he scolded himself as he abruptly turned away from the fountain and made his way to his hotel?

Chapter 3

And all along Nicola had been non-the-wiser, trusting her father's word that she should stick to men from her own culture. Don't bother with tourists, don't come home with an American, it was something he made sure she understood. Being a little girl building big castles in the sky, hoping to one day find her own prince charming, she believed her daddy's outlook on life. And she did exactly what he expected. She only dated Italians, but it so happens that it's the local boys whose eyes wander the moment a woman in a short skirt passes them. Her mother on the other hand always told her to follow her heart, no matter what, but they were both gone now, and she was all alone in a big world with a bunch of conceited, dishonest men who wouldn't think twice to break a woman's heart.

Nicola got ready for bed, tomorrow would be one of those touch and go days. She had to go for her final fitting and hopefully by some miracle her ice cream cravings haven't added any pounds and she would still fit into the dress. By the time her head hit the pillow she fell asleep, she had been too tired to allow Carlos to torment her thoughts.

She ran through the empty streets of Rome, wearing her maid of honor dress, but she had no shoes. She had to find her shoes. She searched everywhere, but she couldn't find them.

"Your shoes are at the fountain," and elderly man said as she passed him by.

"How do you know they are there?"

"You left them there."

The next thing she appeared in the middle of the fountain, water washing down over her, and her shoes dangling from the hands of one of the statues. She tried to jump up to reach them but she was too short. Scanning her surroundings she figured that if she climbed to the top, she could lean over and get them. But then out of the blue, a man stood next to her and effortlessly reached up and unhooked her shoes.

"I believe these are yours?" he said, and a smile tugged at the corners of his mouth.

"Yes, they are, I have no idea how they go there."

"But you left them here," he chuckled and held his hand to help her out of the fountain.

"I swear I didn't!" she protested.

The man started to fade as if he was a ghostly aspiration.

"You have a week to make your wish come true," he whispered.

"Wait!" she called out and as she reached out for him he disappeared into thin air and she tumbled forward.

Nicola woke with a start, her heart beating a million beats a second. It was the strangest dream she had ever had and for a moment it felt so real. She could still feel the cold water penetrating her skin and the touch of the man who helped her get her shoe still burned in the palm of her hand. She was officially going bonkers, she thought as she got out of bed, but as she went to make coffee, she paused at her closet. She had this terrible feeling about those shoes of hers, she hated them but they were for the wedding, and it was only Angelique who would pick such a horrible color for a wedding. She reached for the door handle and hesitated, she was being silly, she thought and withdrew her hand and turned to go to the kitchen. But this persistent feeling of dread that settled in the pit of her stomach, made her turn back to the closet. Taking a deep breath she reached for the closet door and opened it, and immediately relief washed over her. The shoes were still there, bright pink high heeled sandals with glitter all over them. She leaned her head against one of the shelves and closed her eyes. As soon as her obligations as the maid of honor were over, she was going to travel the world, and get a life.

~*~

Posters were plastered all over the walls, calendars with crosses drawn in each day and the words one and week written all over it. Kyle felt his way along the wall, climbing over stored boxes and rubbish that were strewn all over the floor to get to the door. One week, one week, one week, he kept repeating in his mind. The face of the elderly man who approached him at the fountain appeared several times reminding him that he had one week to find the girl. He fought his way through the maze of books and book shelves until he finally reached the door that led him outside, but instead of a cobblestoned path, he was trudging in a stream of water. He had to get out of here, or he was going to go insane. He knew he needed to get to the fountain to take down the pair of shoes the girl left there, and perhaps try to find his Cinderella, but every turn he took just took him further and further away from his final destination.

"This way," the elderly man said as he appeared out of nowhere, "time is running out."

Kyle turned left down a small narrow street and rushed through the darkness to the end where the light drew him closer. The next he knew he was standing on the edge of the fountain, looking at the girl with the bouncy curls and hazel eyes. Finally! He thought and stepped into the fountain.

"I believe these are yours?" he smiled.

"Yes, they are, I have no idea how they go there," she uttered irritably.

"But you left them here," he chuckled as he held his hand for her.

"I swear I didn't!" she protested, but she took his hand, anyway.

The moment they were out of the water, she started to fade.

"You have a week to make your wish come true," she called to him and then shew as gone.

"Wait!" he called out and tried to reach for her, but she was already gone.

By the time Kyle finally woke up he couldn't shake the strange dream he had. The girl he saw tossing coins into the fountain the night before was the very muse of his dream, and the old man he also met was the one who showed him the way. Talk about going nuts, he thought to himself as he dragged himself out of bed. This whole finding love scene was starting to play serious tricks on him.

Chapter 4

Nicola stood in front of the full length mirror while the dress maker took her new measurements and Angelique stood tapping her foot impatiently.

"You know if you run around the block a few times, and just eat carrot sticks and cucumber I'm sure you'll lose the few pounds you've gained."

Nicola rolled her eyes and looked at her reflection in the mirror, "No, I don't have to do anything. This is a sign, don't you see?"

"Utter nonsense," Angelique protested and pushed the assistant out of the way.

"I'm not doing anything, they can just adjust the size," Nicola said adamantly. She was not interested in stopping her ice cream craving over some wedding, she wasn't the bride. Maybe this would teach Angelique a valuable lesson to always have a backup plan.

"Miss Dawson, it's really no trouble, the dress can be adjusted and will fit Miss Morito just fine, I promise," the dressmaker said and smiled reassuringly.

Angelique offered her a friendly smile and shrugged, "That's all good, but come tomorrow she'll have a few more inches we need to consider."

Nicolle huffed and hooked the straps of the dress and shimmied out of it, "Now that's absurd. I came for the dress fitting over three months ago, so it took me that long to gain two pounds. You're so over reacting."

"Fine," Angelique muttered, "I'm just looking out for you. All you need is to show up looking like a beached whale and having Carlos and his new girlfriend laugh at you."

"Ooh, oh that was cruel," Nicola muttered as she tugged on her simple floral print summers dress, "Some friend you are!"

"Nicola, I didn't mean..." Angelique started, but Nichole was already half way out of the boutique.

She felt insulted; the fact that Angelique would be so insensitive towards her was albeit typical. She loved her friend, but sometimes she got too much. Having been more like sisters; quarrels between them erupted often enough but also blew over as soon as it started. But right now she was tired, irritated and completely and utterly upset, and for good reason. She was constantly plagued by silly dreams of romance and one particular stranger, and she had Carlos to face in two days. Angered, she stormed blindly out of the boutique not looking left or right and BANG, straight into a tall soft wall of flesh.

"I'm so sorry!" she apologized, "I wasn't looking where I was head..."

Her mind froze and her words became trapped on the threshold of her lips as she stood back to look up at the man she collided into. He was the same man who she had been dreaming about, from his ruffled sand brown hair, his brown eyes and slightly crooked nose to his broad shoulders and strong arms, not to mention his casual tourist looking attire.

"You, I've..." she started. This was madness! She shook her head mentally and side stepped him, and set off calling over her shoulder, "I'm so sorry!"

"Wait!"

Nicola's heard drummed against her rib cage as if it was trying to escape and although the man called for her to wait, she wouldn't chance it. This was all just too weird.

"Wait, miss!" he called again, and this time she slowed her pace and slowly turned around.

"Have we met before?" he asked as he reached her.

"No we have not," she said, tilting her chin up defiantly. Keep it together Nicola, she warned herself.

"But I'm sure I've seen you before," he insisted, "Look, I'm only here until Saturday, can I at least interest you in some lunch or coffee?"

Over his shoulders she spotted Angelique looking down the road, and she quickly tugged him by his shirt and into the small Bistro, "We can have coffee, as my apology to you for running into you like I did," she said and dragged him to the farthest corner so she could hide from her friend.

~*~

Kyle was completely shocked when the girl from his dreams crashed into him on the sidewalk, but too intrigued to let the moment pass. It was just too much of a coincidence that the same girl who made the wish at the fountain, was the girl in his dreams, and who once gain, stumbled into his life so unexpectedly.

One week. The words kept ringing in his head and on quick calculation there were only two days left before the wish would pass. He dismissed that thought to be a silly old wives tale and pulled out her chair for her to sit down.

"You look upset," he said as he sat down in front of her.

"I am," she muttered, her eyes darting to the door every few seconds.

"Is someone following you?"

"Probably not, I just had to get away from my friend, we had a bit of a quarrel," she said a little more calmly now, "Look I'm sorry I bumped into you like that, if you would order yourself anything off the menu I'll pay for it."

Kyle chuckled and leaned back against the chair, studying her intently. Now that he was up close to her, he realized just how much she looked like the girl in his dreams. The same bouncy curls that flowed freely down over her shoulders were now pinned up on top of her head, exposing her slender neck. Her lips were a bit fuller than he remembered, but it had the same gloss that gave them a slightly cherry pink color.

"My name is Kyle," he murmured as he leaned closer.

"Pardon me," she said looking up, seemingly confused.

"Kyle, my name," he said again and smiled, "Forgive me if I'm completely out of line, but you're breathtaking."

Her sudden intake of breath made him smile, and he looked down to give her time to process it without feeling intimidated.

"Nicola," she whispered and then shifted in her chair, "You asked if we have met before, why do you think we have?"

Well this was going to be interesting, he couldn't exactly tell her that he's been obsessing about a woman he barely knew, or that every night for the past few days, she had been visiting his dreams. He would come across as a complete stalker.

He shrugged, "You just look familiar," he said and then sat back for the waiter to take their order.

After the order was placed, Nicola was the one to talk.

"I know this is going to sound really strange, but I've seen you before too."

"You have?"

She nodded, and picked at a bread stick, "At the Triva Fountain."

"Really, I was there a few nights ago, perhaps that is where I saw you too, you were there with a blond lady and your boyfriend. Now I remember," he admitted.

She wrinkled her nose and pulled a face, "That was Angelique, my friend, she's getting married this Saturday, and that was her fiancé."

Intrigued by that little detail, Kyle felt his heart flutter. So she wasn't taken at all, "Oh, I assumed when he wrapped his arm around you that you were involved."

She shook her head, "He was trying to convince me that going to the wedding was going to be a breeze."

"And you don't want to go?"

She shook her head but did not elaborate. While she sat folding the napkin over and over, flattening the sides nervously he studied her. What if the old man was right, what if they were destined to meet? Was there any truth in the legend of the Trevi Fountain? It was all just too much of a coincidence to ignore.

"Did you find your shoes?" he asked, baiting her to see if it might trigger anything.

"Oh yes, thank you, I have no idea how they got the..." she stopped mid-sentence and whipped her head up, "How did you know about my shoes?"

"Well I'll be damned," he said, completely stunned. She was there too, in his dreams.

"You made a wish in the fountain, and I think somehow it might just have worked."

Nicola looked at him and then stood up, abruptly, "Impossible, wishes don't work, it's a legend that holds no truth."

Kyle stood up at the same time, "Then how do you explain the dream?"

"It's mere chance," she muttered and hooked her bag over her shoulder.

"To such detail?" he insisted, "Your shoes were hooked over the horses' hove and you couldn't reach it."

She didn't respond, just scooted out of and walked hurriedly to the door.

"They were glittery pink," he called after her but she refused to turn around.

"Nicola!" he called but all he was met with, was the jingle of the doorbell and several eyes staring at him.

Chapter 4

Nicola sat at the fountain, her hair neatly tucked under a scarf and wearing sunglasses. Since the day before when she ran into the man from her dreams she had been trying to make sense of it all. The fact that he had known her first dream in such detail was simply too much of a coincidence. Things like that just did not happen, not in real life. And there was also no way that he could have found out about the dream from someone else since she hadn't even told Angelique about her dreams.

She spotted him the moment he came walking past the fountain and took a seat on the opposite side across from her, and she quickly raised the magazine to her face. She lowered it a fraction only to peek over the edge of it. He looked as confused as she did while he fed the pigeons. From where she sat, she had to give it to him, he was handsome as hell and the slight bend on his nose did nothing to spoil his image, in fact it was more like a signature. The only problem was that he was American, and if she dated an American even for fun, her father would turn over in his grave.

"Don't you just love Shakespeare?"

An elderly man who seemed to have appeared out of nowhere said to her as he sat with a book on his lap.

"Unh... yeah, I like Shakespeare," she said half distracted.

"His quotes are remarkable," the man continued, and she just nodded and hummed in agreement.

"It is not in the stars to hold our destiny but in ourselves," he said.

He was really annoying, barging in on her spy time like that, but she hadn't in her to tell him to take a hike either. She had great respect for the elderly, so instead of ignoring him she closed her eyes and took a deep steadying breath.

"Men of few words are the best men," she quoted and closed the magazine on her lap.

"You only have a week to make your wish come true, time is running out," he said quietly next to her.

The words he spoke left her cold, and a shiver ran down her spine, those were almost the exact words Kyle whispered to her in her dreams. Confused she turned to the old man, but he was no longer there. When she looked for Kyle again, he was no longer on the bench.

"One week, that means tomorrow is the last day..." she mumbled to herself.

This was all too strange. She grabbed her handbag and the magazine and as she spun around the heel of her shoe caught in a groove and snapped off.

"Oh snap!" she called out and bent down to pry her broken off heel out from between the stones. This was all she needed. The sun was already starting to set, and her with her luck she would never see Kyle again and her wish would turn to nothing but a collection of dreams. As she made her way back to her house, she felt defeated. She didn't come back to Rome to find love, and here she was, feeling as if her insides were being ripped out and as if she had lost a part of her. She rubbed the palm of her hand with her thumb, where Kyle's hand once touched, and she could feel the heat from his touch resonate through every fiber of her being, but she knew it was going to lead to nothing. He said that he was leaving on Saturday, which meant that she would never see him again. As she reached her apartment and closed the door behind her, she resigned herself to the face that she would one day become a spinster with six cats and a parrot. After this whole escapade with the wishing fountain and the dreams, she would find it hard to give her heart to anyone else.

Chapter 5

Angelique looked exquisite in her wedding dress that was fit for a queen, and as she marched down the aisle towards her future husband, Nicola blinked away a tear. They were two people who were meant to be. Roberto loved her more than he loved life itself, and deep down Nicola wished that she had found such a treasure. She walked behind Angelique, keeping her eyes grounded as they took one step at a time towards the pulpit.

"Nicola," a male voice whispered her name as they passed the guests who sat on either side of the aisle.

She glanced sideways, and the air left her lungs as Kyle stood in one of the seats right next to the aisle. What on earth was he doing here at the wedding; surely he wasn't on the guest list. She glanced at him and smiled awkwardly.

"Will you dance with me?" he whispered again, and she blinked, forcing herself to focus on the task at hand.

Instead of answering him she continued down the aisle behind the bride, and suddenly the feeling of rejection dissipated and her heart fluttered in her chest. She looked up and met Carlos' gaze and was surprised that she didn't recoil or feel inferior at all. In fact, she didn't feel anything. He was just another guest who had no relevance in her life. But from behind her, she could feel Kyle's gaze on her back, and it was as if his very breath was pouring new life into her. For the first time in her life, she felt adored and strangely enough loved. It felt as if she was the most important person in the room.

The wedding ceremony had finally come to an end, and throughout, Nicola had to keep herself from looking for Kyle, but she was aware of him all the time. By the time the guests departed to go to the reception, she was a nervous wreck. Occasionally she had to pinch herself to make sure she was not dreaming again.

When she arrived at the reception with the rest of the brides maids, she was already on the lookout for Kyle. He was nowhere to be seen, and she started to wonder if she had imagined it all. Maybe she was in such a bad state that she was conjuring up these moments out of sheer desperation.

"Nicola!" Angelique called and waved her over, "Can you believe I'm married?"

Nicola smiled and hugged her friend, "Congratulations, I'm sure Roberto will take very good care of you."

"Oh you know he will," Angelique purred as she clung to Roberto's arm.

"Hello Nicola," Carlos piped up next to her.

"Carlos," she said stiffly.

"You look rather dashing today," he tried for small talk, but Nicola was not interested.

"Thank you," she said absentmindedly as she scanned the guests, still looking for any sign of Kyle.

Music filled the room and Roberto twirled his bride into his arms, "It's the opening dance my love," he said and Angelique smiled lovingly up at her husband.

Carlos stepped up and offered his hand to Nicole and she took it without bothering to look at him.

"You seem very distracted," he commented as he rested his hand on the small of her back.

"I'm looking for someone," she said not meeting his eyes.

"I've missed you," he murmured against her ear.

"That's nice," she said.

A few seconds into the song, Carlos tugged her up against him, "You're different," he purred and this time she did look up at him.

"And you haven't changed, now let's get this dance over and done with so that I can be on my merry way," she muttered through clenched teeth and a fake smile.

By the time the song ended she was relieved that she got through it without kicking Kyle in the gut. The song flowed from one into another and Nicola slipped away from Carlos to the edge of the dance floor, planning her great escape. Her duties as the maid of honor was done, and she was no longer needed, besides, Angelique was far too preoccupied with her husband to care where she disappeared to.

"Can I have this dance?" A familiar voice whispered behind her and she spun around.

"Kyle..." she whispered breathlessly, half in shock, "Please tell me that you're not part of my imagination?"

He chuckled and wrapped his arm around her waist, resting her one hand in the palm of his hand as he led her on to the dance floor, "I keep asking myself the very same thing," he said.

Nicola looked up at him and smiled softly, "If this is a dream, I'd rather stay asleep," she whispered.

"I can assure you it's not a dream, but if you want, I can pinch you to test the theory," he joked.

"Trust me, I've been pinching myself since the very first day you snuck into my dreams," she said and looked lovingly up into his eyes.

"Likewise," he whispered.

Everything around her faded to nothing, all that mattered were the two of them and as Kyle lowered his lips to hers and kissed her, she surrendered to him. They were two souls who were lost to each other and all it had taken was a simple wish to spur destiny on and draw them together.

~*~

Miniel, the angel who induces love, stood on the upper level balcony and looked down at the loving couple and smiled. His work was done until he was called for the next intervention.

"Love sought is good, but given unsought, is better."
~William Shakespeare~

REACH FOR HIM

SARAH LOVE

Bridget Perry flipped down the visor against the afternoon sun as she steered in sweeping curves along the coastal road. She drew in her breath sharply. Her wrists hurt. She glanced at her wrists which were bruised and swollen and then averted her eyes. She didn't want to be reminded of them or of the event that caused them.

For the umpteenth time that day, tears welled in her eyes and spilled down her cheeks. Not even the stunning beauty of an Australian sunset could distract her from the heaviness in her heart. Images of her ex, came unbidden to her mind; his fathomless black eyes and raven hair falling long and wavy down his muscled back; his teeth white against swarthy skin. Bridget's breath caught in her throat. "Jackson," she whispered through her tears. She sighed one long shuddering miserable breath. Why was she crying over that two-timing, heartless pig anyway? Because I don't know how to be by myself, was the honest answer.

Bridget squinted and slowed down. With the sun at this angle she could barely see a few feet in front of her. She rounded the bend at a crawl and noticed a small motel sitting back away from the road, shrouded in thick foliage; a wooden sign peeped out from behind a heavy overhang of magenta flowers; Bougainvillea lodge it said in a cursive blue letters. Suddenly, Bridget wanted nothing more than to stop at here away from the sun, where she would be able to rest and recuperate. She pulled in and the gravel crunched in welcome as she parked the car. She stifled a groan. Sitting in the car for fourteen hours straight had done its work on her muscles. As she pulled herself out of the car and stretched her arms behind her head, she caught a glimpse of the view. Bougainvillea lodge had a perfect position facing the beach, which was, to her great relief, devoid of crowds, except for a lone walker and his dog and a young couple with small children paddling in the shallows.

The woman behind the counter welcomed her with just the right balance of warmth and respect for privacy that she needed, giving her a key and reminding her that dinner would be served at the restaurant at six. With slow deliberate steps, Bridget carried her bag, packed in such haste the night before and now she realized depressingly light, to her room. Not doubting that she had left most of her best clothes and belongings behind, she looked around the room. Nothing special, she thought, but adequate for her needs. The bathroom looked clean enough and turning back the bed, she was pleased to find crisp white cotton sheets. Right now that was all the mattered, a hot shower and sleep.

With her clothes strewn across the bathroom floor, she winced with pleasure as the hot water pummelled her tired and sore shoulders. She lathered up every part of her body and scrubbed. What she was scrubbing away she wasn't sure, but the need to be clean was overwhelming. There was more crying, but this time, the tears were more from relief than sadness. It felt good to be alone where no one could reach her or find her. She was so tired. It was all she could do to dry herself off and pull on some clean underwear and a t-shirt and crawl, exhausted into bed.

When she opened her eyes the room was dark with one brilliant shard of light spilling through a gap in the heavy drapes. Bridget reached out and felt her way over the bedside table for her phone. Her home screen glowed with a photo of Jackson during their holiday to Bali the year before. She frowned at it and focused on the time instead – 11.am! She flopped back on the pillows for a minute, amazed at how long she had slept. She lay there listening to her body. She felt relaxed and for the first time in ten months, safe.

Last April, Jackson had walked into her life and turned it upside down. He was mesmerizing in his masculine beauty. She was the envy of women wherever they went; she saw it in their eyes. Women, who ordinarily were shy and mousey, became predatory and catlike in his presence. He was talented, funny, and charming in public; but it hadn't taken long for her to realize that behind closed doors he was a cold, narcissistic bully. Ten months of verbal put-downs had left her believing that no other man would ever tolerate her the way he did. She had suspected cheating but had never been able to find any definitive evidence. He didn't need to cheat behind her back anyway. He was happy enough to flirt with other women right under her nose. On the rare occasion she called him out on it, he would jeer and tell her she was lucky to be with him and to leave if she didn't like it.

She didn't like it, but she didn't dare leave. Her best friend Nick had voiced his disapproval over and over. The image of him clenching his large, usually gentle, hands in frustration, came to mind. Dear, loyal Nick, with his lanky frame, round blue eyes, and freckled upturned nose, exactly the same as it had been when they played together as five-year-olds. He had always been there and she couldn't imagine the world without him in it. Some people winked and hinted that they would one day end up together, but she had always laughed at the idea. Nick was so safe. She knew him possibly better than she knew herself sometimes and she wanted mystery and adventure. As a result, her attention was too readily arrested by men who were exciting and unavailable in some way.

"It ticks me off," Nick had grumbled one day a few weeks into her relationship with Jackson. They were sitting on her couch watching re-runs of Seinfeld and eating chips.

"What ticks you off?"

"You, and other women too, always gushing slavishly over wankers like Jackass, I mean Jackson." He smiled wickedly. "What is it with women and bad boys? Do you actually want to be treated like crap?"

Bridget threw a cushion at Nick's head messing up the top of his straight brown hair. "He's not that bad!" She dodged the cushion on its return flight. "I don't know why but there's just something irresistible about a man who might not hang around. Knowing that he might go, but he's choosing to stay with me is sort of exciting, y'know?"

Nick's expression was incredulous. "No, I don't know! Bridge' that's the most ludicrous idea. The guy doesn't care about you! He puts you down! People don't do that to people they love, can't you see that?"

"He's had a rough life!" she countered. "His dad was a deadbeat. His mom had different men parading through his childhood. He didn't get shown much love and I want to make up for that. I think I can heal him if I love him enough."

Nick had stared at her long and hard, finally pulling her to him in a warm hug. "That isn't love Bridget. That's not how love works. Love isn't a one-way thing. It's like water." He pulled back and looked Bridget in the face. "Love is like water and people are like sponges. If you pour love into someone they should soak it up like a sponge, but if a person is like a rock, then the love just splashes and runs off the side getting wasted on the ground. Jackson's heart is a rock. You're wasting your love on him."

He had gone home after that and Bridget had thought about his analogy many times since then. It had all come to a head when last night after work, she had gone into their bathroom and found a woman's earring in the sink. She had confronted Jackson about it when he got home drunk in the early hours of the next morning, and instead of lying or being ashamed, he had mocked her and told her that the earring woman was here to stay and she could take it or leave it. She had screamed and thrown herself at him in a panicked rage and that was when he had grabbed her by the wrists twisting them cruelly and making her sink to the floor, a defeated wreck. She had packed a hurried bag and left there and then, not thinking or looking back and now 30 hours later she was here, alone, and finally free.

Pulling back the drapes of her motel room revealed a glorious Summer's day. From her window, the water glistened and the sand glowed white in the sun. It was much busier today. What had seemed like an empty country road the night before was now fringed with parked cars baking in the heat. Families strolled up and down and from the beach; the sounds of laughter and excited yelps carried across to her window.

Bridget threw on a pair of lavender shorts and a white cheesecloth peasant blouse. She looked at herself critically in the mirror. Her eyes still had a residue of puffiness from all the crying and over-sleeping but she didn't feel like wearing make-up. Her face stared back at her in solemn comradery. At 27, Bridget could still boast clear, olive skin with a smattering of freckles. Her best features apparently, were her large hazel eyes and long auburn hair. She curled her lip; obviously, Jackson didn't think they were that great. Before she could let her thoughts wander gloomily down that road, she pulled herself away from the mirror, grabbed her bag and left the room.

The air was balmy on her skin and the sound of her sandals slapping against the cool tiles brought a delicious sensation of Summer holidays bubbling up inside her. It seemed like the real Bridget was struggling up in revolt against the old, Jackson oppressed, Bridget, desperate to make a comeback. The lady behind the desk welcomed her with a smile.

"Nice day for it," she beamed. "Heading down to the beach?"

"Yep, just going for a stroll. It's busier than I expected it to be."

"That's because the agricultural show is on in Bluegum this week. When people get too hot traipsing around the showgrounds they inevitably end up here at Opal Bay to cool off. Are you going to the show today?"

Bridget let her mind wander for a moment. She imagined the showgrounds packed with hot sweaty people, crying children, loud music, and smelly livestock. She shook her head, smiling. "No, I think I'll just enjoy a peaceful day on the beach, thanks. How much are those straw hats?"

"That'll put you back ten dollars, love."

Bridget chose a broad-brimmed straw hat with a yellow and white polka-dot band. As she closed the door of the reception office behind her, she was hit with a wall of heat. In the scramble of departure, she hadn't thought to pack things like sunscreen. Without it, she was going to end the day red as a lobster, but throwing caution to the wind, she stepped out into the day with a 'come what may' attitude. She followed the sounds of laughter, seagulls, and surf across the road and through a scrubby pathway cut through the sand, slowing down against the resistance of the sand, panting a little at the effort. A couple of pre-teen boys hurtled past her, laughing like hyenas. They missed her by inches, covering her with sand in the process. She laughed out loud. She couldn't be angry. Their innocence was unapologetically refreshing.

An enticing aroma wafted over to her from a food stand that had been set up on the beach under a canopy. It was a sausage sizzle. Bridget's stomach growled; she hadn't given food a second thought since leaving Jackson, and now, all of a sudden, she felt that she could devour an entire side of beef. Two long lines of hungry beachgoers had formed at the stand, so Bridget took her place behind an elderly woman baked brown and wrinkled from a lifetime spent on Aussie beaches. Everyone was buying as much as they could in one go, and the line was moving slowly, so Bridget found herself watching the other people in the queue.

In the line next to her and a few places ahead, a tall person caught her eye. Bleached blond hair over a pair of broad tanned shoulders, tapering down to slim hips in turquoise board shorts made her smile in appreciation. She hoped he would turn around so that she could see his face. Come on, she urged mentally, turn around just a little bit. As if he heard her thoughts, the tall man turned and looked straight at her with startling blue eyes. He held her gaze just for a second and then turned back. Bridget felt like she had been hit by a sledgehammer. A very gorgeous, beach-babe kind of sledgehammer. "Just like Captain America," she murmured inwardly.

"You're too right about that, love."

Startled, Bridget looked down to see the old lady beaming up at her. "Did I say that out loud?" she gasped, mortified.

"Yeah, but who could blame you?" The old lady looked dreamily over at the handsome man and sighed. "If I was fifty years younger, he'd be in trouble, that's all I can say."

Bridget giggled and chatted with the old lady until at last, she got to the top of the line and bought her food which she ate at the base of some dunes further up the beach. Every now and then she would search the water to locate the tall blond. He was easy to spot in his turquoise board shorts out in the surf catching a few waves. It was nice to watch him unobserved from her vantage point. Occasionally, she would acknowledge a twinge of guilt over looking at a man other than Jackson, and then the truth would come slamming down like a judge's gavel. Verdict - Jackson isn't yours, Bridget. He never was. He doesn't love you. It's over. Then the real Bridget would push again from within. The indignant Bridget, the proud Bridget, encouraging and boosting her confidence a smidgen further. It was a sensation she welcomed back with open arms.

From her spot on the beach, the sapphire-blue water looked so tempting, she regretted not bringing something to swim in. But there was no reason not to get at least a little bit wet. She unfolded her stiff muscles and made her way down to the water's edge, wading in till the water came up to her knees. Keeping to the shallows, Bridget splashed along, stopping here and there to pick up a pretty shell which she tucked into the pocket of her shorts. An urgent shout somewhere behind her, made Bridget turn around. Further back where she had been sitting, a woman was screaming for help. Some people were stopping and looking at her with concern. Although Bridget couldn't hear, she could see they were asking her what was the matter. Others, Bridget noticed in angry amazement, had pulled their phones out and were recording the scene. And then Bridget saw it, at the woman's feet, a small limp body lay in the sand. Without a second thought, Bridget started to run. Where were the lifeguards? She'd seen their watch tower about five hundred meters up the beach. As she ran, she shouted at anyone who would listen. "Call the lifeguards! Unconscious child on the beach!" Bridget fell momentarily and was up in an instant, sprinting as hard as her legs would carry her. Out of the corner of her eye, another figure was running up from the water. It was Turquoise board shorts, hurtling along like some kind of superhero toward the screaming woman. Bridget arrived panting heavily at the woman's side. What she saw made her heart sink.

"My boy! Help my boy! A Bluebottle stung him. I think he's allergic!"

Without answering, Bridget sank to her knees by the little boy. He looked about five and his lips were blue. Across his torso and upper arms were the tell-tale red welts of a jellyfish sting. Bluebottles were painful but not usually dangerous. If this child was experiencing anaphylactic shock, he could die. She shouted again for someone to get the lifeguards and then, summoning everything she had learned in First Aid at school, she immediately began CPR. Beside her, the boy's mother was kneeling over them now with silent tears coursing down her face. Bridget was also aware of Turquoise board shorts beside her assessing the situation.

"What's going on? Are you trained?" he was asking Bridget. She shook her head.

"Bluebottle sting. Possible allergic reaction."

"Then let me help; you breathe; I'll do the compressions."

Together, the two of them continued to work on the little boy with the hushed, expectant crowd watching on. Bridget wondered if they were making any difference at all when finally, after what seemed an age, the crowd parted for two lifeguards, who quickly assessed the situation, and took over. Relieved, Bridget and Turquoise board shorts, moved away, shaking and exhausted from the adrenaline coursing through their veins. They stood leaning on each other watching on as the lifeguards worked. Bridget found herself praying repeatedly; please God, don't let him die? The silence around them was heavy, broken only by the sounds of the lifeguards working on the little boy and the mournful call of gulls. The waves rolled into shore rhythmically as though they were trying to drum life back into the child.

A sudden noise split the quiet. A wet splutter and a weak cough, and then thank heaven, a louder choke and cough, and then a cry! An unearthly wail burst from the little boy's mother as she realized her son wasn't dead and a cheer rose from the crowd. Bridget found herself turning to congratulate Turquoise board shorts only to find that he had left. When did that happen? She scanned the beach without success. He was nowhere to be seen. Bridget turned back to watch the little boy being carried off on a stretcher. His mother paused a moment to hug her and thank her.

"Thank you so much, I think you saved my little boy's life! Please thank your boyfriend for me okay?" She hurried off to follow her son and the crowd dispersed. Bridget stood there, suddenly deflated after the intensity of the experience. For some reason, the beach had lost its attraction and her thoughts turned to the Agricultural show. Maybe it wouldn't be such a bad idea to go for an hour or two?

Half an hour later she was entering the town of Bluegum having first gone back to the motel for a change of clothes. It was easy to find the showgrounds. Street signs directing the traffic to the show were on every corner. Pedestrians seemed to have only one destination, and when she pulled into carpark she could see that there was still a bit of a queue to buy tickets. Bridget entered the grounds through an old-fashioned turnstile joining the throng of hot and tired patrons trying to navigate the crowds. The festival was in full swing with Ferris wheels and Dodgem cars, side shows, and fairy floss stands. She passed huge barns and stables which housed all of the prize winning livestock. The smell of manure wafted out making Bridget's nostrils twitch. Ugh, she thought, immediately regretting her decision. What she needed was somewhere she could just sit and be entertained for a while. Reflecting on childhood visits to the Royal Melbourne Show, a particularly fond memory popped into her head. The Grand Arena, of course! She would go and watch the parades of animals, the horse tricks, the clowns and daredevil acts and maybe even wait till evening for the firework display.

Bridget decided to just follow the general flow of pedestrians, stopping here and there to look at displays on the way. On the corner of an intersection was an old fashioned American style diner where they sold snacks and takeaway food. As she passed she could see into the diner. People were sitting, chatting and eating in the leather upholstered booths. She was hungry, but she wasn't in the mood for hotdogs. She was just about to cross the road and stop at a place selling kebabs when out of the corner of her eye she glimpsed a flash of blond hair. Bridget stopped dead in her tracks causing a man and woman to crash into her from behind.

"Watch where you're bloody going!"

Bridget wasn't sure if she apologized or not. She actually didn't care, because there, shoving a hot dog into his beautiful mouth, was Turquoise board shorts, in the American Diner! Before embarrassment, fear, or good judgment could stop her, she had climbed the few steps and walked through the glass doors. He didn't look up; he was too engrossed in his meal to notice. Bridget found herself standing by his booth with a shy grin on her face.

"Hi."

Turquoise board shorts started. His wide blue eyes opening even wider at the sight of her. "Hey!" He struggled to stand up but got hooked up on the corner of the table, jabbing his hip and making him wince. He smiled through the pain, extending his hand to her. "Hey, it's you, the CPR girl!"

"Yep, it's me. I was just passing and happened to see you. You left so quickly at the beach, I was hoping to introduce myself and thank you for your help... do you mind if I join you?"

"No, not at all, no worries, I'd enjoy you... I mean, that would be nice."

Bridget slid into the booth across from him and they appraised each other for a couple of seconds.

"I'm Bridget, and you are?"

"Daniel, Daniel Inglis."

"You say that like you're James Bond or something." Bridget ran her hand through her hair and twiddled with a loose curl at the end. "Actually, you did look a bit like James Bond running up the beach like that to save the day."

Daniel grimaced. "Oh, no, did I? How embarrassing. Well, you were doing a bit of a Wonder woman yourself. It was quite impressive."

Bridget laughed. "We should have our own show!" They were interrupted by a waitress who took Bridget's order. Bridget continued, "So, do you live locally?"

"No." Just on a trip for work and passing through. You?"

Bridget sighed, wondering how much she should say. "No, I'm not local. I guess you could say I'm a city girl looking to make a sea change. I'm on the hunt for a new place to establish some roots and start a new life." She stopped wondering if she had said too much. Daniel seemed to understand and didn't pry any further.

"That sounds quite an appealing idea actually. I think we all could benefit from starting afresh once in a while. What do you do for a crust?"

"I'm a teacher, and I run an online business writing résumés and cover letters." She narrowed her eyes at him, thinking. "Hmm, let me see if I can guess what you are. You look like you could be a doctor... am I close?"

"Well, I am in the business of taking care of people so you're right there. I guess you could say I'm a social worker of sorts."

Bridget absorbed the information in happy disbelief; this guy was almost too good to be true. A social worker meant he was someone who cared about people, not only that, he was polite, unpretentious, and of course drop dead gorgeous. And the best thing about him, she decided, was that he was the absolute opposite of Jackson. All of the feelings of longing and hurt about Jackson dissolved right there in that diner booth. It fizzled into nothing so quickly she was shocked into stark realization of what she had been succumbing herself to for the past ten months. The understanding that not only had Jackson never loved her but that she had never loved him was as plain as the nose on her face. Across from her Daniel was looking at her with one eyebrow raised and a crooked smile.

"By the look on your face, my job description doesn't meet with your approval."

"What? Oh, no! I think it's a wonderful, honorable kind of work... No, if I looked odd, I was thinking of how different you are to someone I know."

Daniel was quiet, focusing his attention on removing the cherry from the top of his Ice-cream Sundae. It slipped off the edge of his spoon and slid down the side of his glass onto the plate; his eyes traveled from his plate to the bruises on her wrists. "Is that someone you're running away from?" His blue eyes looked up and held her in a questioning gaze for a moment before licking the ice-cream off his spoon. Bridget pulled her hands back under the table, her voice was mildly indignant.

"You could say that. But not running. Yesterday I was dragging myself away, but today I can say it's over. I've left and I'm never going back."

"Good."

Bridget looked up at him. He was looking at her steadily, knowingly. She took a deep breath. "And now I'm all alone like Nellie No Friends at the Bluegum Agricultural Show. I don't suppose I could twist your arm to spend the day with me? I'd feel silly going on the roller coaster by myself."

Daniel hesitated, but only for an instant. "Consider it twisted," he said with a grin.

They spent the rest of the afternoon having more fun than Bridget had experienced in what seemed like years. Daniel was funny and intelligent and insightful with an air of confidence that was deeply appealing. Never once did he utter a sexist remark or blurt obscenities or look her over like a piece of steak, like Jackson would have. In contrast, he was the consummate gentleman, helping her onto rides, walking ahead of her in the crowds to shield her from being jostled, and opening doors for her. Once or twice when standing in a queue she would feel his hand brush against hers or his hand on her arm protectively.

After the sun went down, they took their dinner to the Grand Arena to watch the fireworks. As they stood staring mesmerized like little children at the display, Bridget felt Daniel's arms slip around her waist from behind. She leaned into him, enjoying the hard warmth of his chest against her back and his mouth near her ear. Like this, it was difficult to concentrate on the fireworks because there were fireworks of another sort going off inside her. But, fighting to the surface of her consciousness, a small voice came unsolicited from the deepest recesses of her mind. It was a voice of – what was it a voice of, caution perhaps, or was it good judgment? Don't rush it was telling her, but the voice quickly became garbled and indistinct as she pushed it back where it came from.

Their conversation became slower and quieter after that. A different kind of language had taken over. Words were replaced by holding hands and shy caresses. As they walked back to Daniel's car the air was electric with the question – what next? There was a choice to be made. Was Daniel making the same choice? What was he thinking? She looked at him sideways out of the corner of her eye, as he fumbled with the car keys. He's nervous too, she realized. The trip home in the car was silent except for snippets of polite small talk. Neither of them wanted to destroy the mood, they were heading toward one conclusion for the night and they both knew it.

Daniel walked Bridget to her door; the light above had blown and they were standing, conveniently, in the shadows, away from prying eyes. She wondered if there was any point going through the usual end of date etiquette of thanking Daniel for a nice time, the invitation for a nightcap etc. He was still behind her, so she turned to face him and lifted her face to his. What she saw on his face startled her somewhat. His eyes that had been bright and blue all day, were now almost black; his pupils dilated to their fullest. There was an intensity there that both frightened her and bound her, unable to look away. She ran her tongue over her lips in anticipation and his eyes dropped to her mouth. When he spoke, his voice was hoarse.

"You have the most beautiful mouth."

Bridget's lips curled into a softly parted smile and she leaned in closer. He was going to kiss her. She closed her eyes and waited, focusing all of her attention on her mouth in anticipation. The night breeze on her moist lips was cool, and then his lips were there, warm, firm and full on hers. His arms went around her and lifted her up so that her toes were barely touching the ground. He held her so effortlessly that she let herself relax into the kiss. This was more like it; so much nicer than Jackson's hurried, rough embraces. A new idea came to her mind, wouldn't it be nice to leave it here and to let it remain sweet and romantic, to softly say goodnight and close the door in anticipation of another date? But as Daniel's kisses became more urgent, her resolve began to weaken. Self-control had never been her forte. She broke the kiss and pulled away. "Stay with me?" she whispered. Daniel nodded and followed her into the dark motel room and closed the door behind him with a click.

She was in a strange house with a corridor flanked by walls with garish lime wallpaper. The color made her nauseous. Along the walls were dozens of doors leading to dark rooms, which she entered panicked and fevered, looking for something, but she didn't know what. "I'm running out of time, running out of time!" The words ran in a loop over and over in her head, but the further she ran down the corridor the smaller it got and every room became more cramped, stifling her and filling her with desperate dread, until finally she was wedged tight and suffocating at the pointed end of the corridor, curled up in a ball.

Bridget woke with a start sitting bolt upright in the dawn light, covered in perspiration and her chest heaving. The dream, which was a reoccurring one, was still fresh in her mind, but she knew if she waited a minute it would fade. Then she remembered Daniel. Jerking her head around, she stared at the other side of the bed. It was rumpled, but empty. She scanned the room. He was gone. He had left nothing behind. A small white object on the sheet beside her caught her eye. It was the butt of a ticket for the roller coaster ride from the day before. Bridget lay back on the pillow staring with unseeing eyes at the tiny shred of paper. Last night had not been what she had expected. She had expected to wake up full and replete with Prince Charming breathing softly beside her. Instead, the experience had been furtive and intense. Daniel's set jaw and black eyes swam before her. There had been nothing magical about last night as she had hoped. A ball of regret began to form in the pit of her stomach. It was too soon after Jackson. She had known that last night. Why couldn't she just say no to men? Nick was going to have something to say about this when she told him.

The thought of unburdening herself to Nick gave her some comfort. The red digits on the bedside clock glowed 6:23; a bit early but he'd be getting up to get ready for work soon anyway. His phone rang out. She was hesitating, wondering whether she should try again when her phone began to vibrate; Nick's photo coming up on her screen. She swiped the screen with relief.

"Hi, it's me." Nick's voice was heavy with sleep.

"Hi, me, sorry for waking you up. I just needed to talk to my best mate."

"Hmm. Are you okay?"

Bridget could hear him yawning and stretching on the other end of the line.

"Yeah, I'm safe but just depressed and sick of myself. I'm so stupid, Nick."

"What happened?"

"I met this guy."

Nick moaned in exasperation. "What? A guy? Bridget, it has been three days since you left Jackson. Three days! You have no business getting involved with any guy for any reason right now. And then, realizing that he hadn't heard her out, his tone softened. "I'm sorry, I didn't give you a chance to explain, go ahead."

"No, you are right to be exasperated. I met a guy, a really nice guy, but I rushed things and he ended up staying the night. He didn't hurt me, it's not like he's a serial killer or anything, I just feel stupid for being so desperate and having no self-control." Her voice began to quiver with emotion. "I've forgotten what's good about me, Nick. I'm just sick of myself."

Nick didn't answer right away and when he did his voice was tender. "There's plenty that's good about you Bridget." But you have to learn how to be alone and happy before you can be with someone and be happy. There are good men out there, but you have to be willing to change your expectations. My mom always said that the best apples were at the top of the tree and the hardest ones to find and she was right." The silence on Bridget's end told Daniel she was crying. "You're the best friend I've ever had Bridget and I hate to see you sad. I think you're crazy sometimes, but I'll always be here for you. What are you going to do now? Will you come home?"

A part of Bridget wanted to go home, but she had left for a reason, to learn about herself and to reinvent herself where nobody had any preconceived notions about her. "No Nick. I'm going to find somewhere to settle up here and make a go of it. Thanks for listening to me, you're my bestie and I love you." Nick's voice was soft in reply. "I love you too."

Once Bridget was dressed, she went into Bluegum and bought some supplies, including a map of Queensland. Her motel room had been cleaned and the bed made when she returned. It matched her mood. She felt energized. It was finally time to leave her old life and her old mistakes behind her. But she needed a place to lay down roots. She spread the map out over the small circular dining table, holding it in place with the pepper and salt shakers on two corners and the sugar bowl on another. She rummaged in her shopping bag and ripped open a crackling plastic package containing a brand new red felt pen. She leaned close to locate Bluegum on the map and placed a small red dot there, then, raising the pen like a dagger, she shut her eyes and dropped her arm, randomly onto the map. It had landed about two inches away from the Bluegum dot. "Good, not too far to drive then," she muttered. She squinted and shifted her head to the side to see the name of her new hometown. Currawong about an hour away from Bluegum. She liked the name of the town immediately. Currawong, one of her favourite Australian birds, like a large black crow with patches of white on the tips of its wings was a good omen to her. She had no idea what was at Currawong, maybe she would arrive to find nothing, but she was going to go anyway and see what happened.

The trip was uneventful, but as she drew closer to her destination, she was pleased to see green fields, rather than the harsh yellow bushlands she had been expecting. A large sign on the side of the road said: "You are entering Currawong – pop 5000." She instantly felt like she had gone back 60 years. The houses were vintage weatherboard houses, circa 1950 with immaculate gardens and pristine driveways. Many of the homes were on acreage with a couple of horses grazing back from the road. The main strip was fairly modern but it only took a few minutes to drive through the center of town and then she was back out in the country.

Being careful to keep to the speed limit, she headed for the motel she had booked into back in Opal Bay. "Turn left in 100 meters," said the ever polite voice on her GPS. As Bridget turned left she admired a sweet old bluestone church on the corner. A group of parishioners were in the front weeding and tending the garden. They were an assorted group of moms, dads, children, teenagers and old age pensioners, all working together in a steady rhythm. With her windows rolled down, she could hear laughter and chatter coming from the group. Something inside her wished she could park the car and join in; there seemed to be such a spirit of belonging amongst them.

That night as she lay in her motel bed, looking through the newspaper for rental properties, she reflected on the little church again. As a little girl, her parents had taken her every week to church and she had enjoyed their time together as a family. She remembered the solemn feelings she held in her heart, even as a child, for the church and everything it stood for. She missed the reverent prayers, the quiet atmosphere, and the hope it all inspired. Maybe that was what was missing in her life? How far had she drifted away from her core beliefs? How much had she let the whims and wishes of others influence her away from what she held to be true? She made the decision there and then, that she would attend church services the next Sunday. Bridget felt much lighter over the next couple of days. She felt good about looking inside herself and facing her demons head on. It was nice to let the misery go and to commit to change. It felt like her soul was being washed clean in her resolve to be happy.

On Sunday morning, she dressed for church. Her packing had been abysmal with absolutely nothing that could pass as suitable for church, so the day before, she had bought herself a new dress befitting her mood. It was a crisp cotton dress with a fitted bodice and wide knee-length skirt in pale yellow. She matched it with a pair of summery slingback white stilettos and finished the look by pulling her auburn hair up into a long ponytail, making her look every bit as wholesome as she hoped she would. Looking herself over in the mirror she raised an eyebrow at her reflection. "This is it, Bridget. Don't let me down."

The walk to church seemed to be straight out of a Disney movie. The sun was shining, the birds singing, the breeze cool and refreshing. Families were walking to church together in their Sunday best. Bridget held back a little. She wanted to be the last to walk into the chapel so that she wouldn't be an object of curiosity to the others. At first, when she entered the chapel she was blinded in the cool dark after the brilliance of the outside sunshine. The chapel was nearly full friends and families in soft conversation, waiting for the reverend to emerge from the vestry. Bridget quietly took a seat in the last pew. Thankfully nobody had noticed her yet. She sat in quiet meditation, while the organist treated them to soft prelude music. It was rare that Bridget felt confident about one of her decisions, but today, she was convinced she was in the right place.

The prelude music faded and the congregation turned their faces in unison toward the vestry door. A soft click of a door latch at the side of the chapel released a beam of yellow light from within and emerging from the light, a tall figure, so tall and broad he had to bend his head to avoid hitting the top of the door. It was a blond head. From where she sat, Bridget couldn't see his face, only the back of his blond head and his black robes. Bridget's heart began to beat quicker. There was an uncomfortable sensation bubbling up from her stomach to her throat. The reverend was looking far too familiar for her liking. Then as the organist began to play the opening hymn, he turned around to face the congregation. Bridget took an audible gasp of air. Daniel! It was Daniel!

The congregation rose from their seats in a synchronized swoosh. Somewhere on the right side of the chapel, someone dropped their hymnbook with a loud clatter, but Bridget barely heard it; the chorus of voices around her was a muffled behind the blood whooshing through her ears. She felt faint and leaned forward to rest her head on the back of the pew in front of her. Daniel, a priest? Shame and anger threatened to drown her as she remembered with embarrassment their night together. If she'd known, she would have never.... How dare he not tell her? The shame began to dissipate. He was the one breaking his vows. She wasn't party to that. She looked up at him standing at the pulpit. Was he going to stand up there and preach from the Bible now?

The hymn ended and the congregation sat, waving fans in the heat, all eyes watching Daniel in rapt expectation. Bridget was glad that the chapel was full. It was unlikely that Daniel would see her sitting down in the back row, but leaving was out of the question; firstly, he would see her leave and think her a coward and secondly, she wanted to confront him. He started to speak and Bridget, in spite of herself was impressed. He wasn't preachy at all. He spoke of kindness and acceptance, service and dedication. He told amusing anecdotes that made the congregation chuckle, he mentioned people by name, he spoke of his own weaknesses. Bridget was starting to soften. Maybe the night with her was a one-off? Maybe, like everyone else, he had weaknesses that he was trying to work through? As the hour passed, so did her indignation. She gazed at Daniel. He was beautiful she had to admit. Maybe there could be a future with him? If she were to approach him and if he were willing, they could start afresh, and she would never ask him to overstep the boundaries of his faith. Nick's words nagged at her conscience, "you have to learn to be alone." "Oh, shut up, Nick," she mumbled out loud, making the people in front of her turn and stare.

After the service, Bridget, made her way against the stream of people leaving the chapel, up towards the pulpit, where Daniel was tidying up and preparing to leave. She arrived at the front just as he was heading towards the vestry.

"Reverend Inglis?"

Daniel turned swiftly with a ready smile, which fell comically as soon as he recognized her. "Yes? Oh!"

"Surprised to see me?"

Daniel's face froze into a stiff smile, but his eyes were boring into hers heavy with meaning. He spoke in urgent tones through his stiff smile like a ventriloquist. "Can't talk now." He glanced over Bridget's shoulder at someone approaching from behind. And then she heard the sound that made her blood run cold; a little girl's voice over the din of the departing congregation.

"Daddy!"

Like an ax dropping onto the executioner's block, Bridget's expression dropped into one of quiet fury. Not this. There would be no forgiving for this! She looked over her shoulder to see a little girl of about four, with honey colored curls running toward Daniel. He stood stiffly as his daughter hugged his legs. Following the little girl was a dark haired woman with a babe in arms. The woman approached her with a friendly smile. "Hello, you must be new? I'm Carrie Inglis, welcome!" She offered her hand to Bridget who did her best to hitch a believable looking smile onto her face. Whatever had happened was not this woman's fault, and she was not going to do anything that could possibly hurt her any further. "Hi, Carrie, nice to meet you."

Carrie's face was open, gazing directly into Bridget's eyes. "It's always good to have new people join us," she turned to Daniel, "isn't it honey?" But Daniel was already half way out of the chapel with his little girl in tow. Carrie laughed. "What's his rush? He's usually hanging around talking for ages after church. So, tell me about yourself, where are you staying?" She was so genuine that Bridget found herself wavering between shock and anger at Daniel and an irresistible connection with his wife. Overriding these two emotions was an overwhelming desire to get away, to be alone where she could lick her wounds and somehow come to terms with what had happened. She jotted down her address and phone number for Carrie and then making her excuses she made her way back to the motel room. It wasn't until she was alone that the full impact of what Daniel had subjected her to hit her. All of the excuses she had tried to make for him, fell flat and lifeless. He was a liar and a cheater and cheating on one of the loveliest ladies she had ever met and only a few weeks after she'd given birth to a new baby!

Like the voice of her conscience sitting on her shoulder, Nick's voice came to her mind. "It takes two to tango," he was saying, "Daniel didn't do this on his own."

"But I didn't know he was married!" she cried out to the room at large. "Did you know anything about him before you invited him home?" came Nick's steady voice again.

Bridget looked at her phone. If she had Nick's voice berating her in her head, she may as well call him and get the confession over and done with. He was going to find out about this at some point anyway, and she really needed his advice. When he answered his voice was cautious but hopeful.

"Hey Bridget, is this call to just say hi to your best friend because you miss me, or have you got bad news?"

Bridget sighed. "Bad news. He is a priest. A married priest with two children."

"Who, what? No, not the guy from the other night? How do you know?"

"I randomly attended his church today. How's that for serendipity?"

There was silence on the line for a moment. "Maybe serendipity, or maybe a life lesson? Maybe a chance to make things right? Wow, Bridge' what a shock. What's his wife like? Did she find out?"

"She's an absolute darling. Anybody who could willingly hurt a person like her has got to have something wrong with them, and no, thankfully, she doesn't know anything."

"What are you going to do?"

Bridget asked herself the same question. What was she going to do? She felt she had been directed to this little town, and directed to the church. Should she let Daniel's presence influence her own journey? No, why should he have a say? Maybe Currawong had happier surprises up its sleeve for her. The decision formed and settled in her heart. "I'm going to stay," she answered.

The week that followed was a blur. Carrie contacted her on the Tuesday with a fabulous rental opportunity. An elderly aunt and uncle were going overseas for six months and needed a house-sitter. The situation was perfect, she wouldn't have to buy furniture, the rent was cheap and the house boasted a backyard shady with glorious, mauve, Jacarandas and a wrap-around veranda, perfect for entertaining or working on her laptop. By Thursday she had moved in and made friends with neighbors and been invited for tea. By 10 o'clock that evening she was brushing her teeth getting ready for bed and feeling appreciative and hopeful for the future.

She had just pulled on an old t-shirt and a pair of Jackson's old boxers when she heard what she thought was a quiet knock on the front door. She stopped and cocked an ear to listen. Who would be knocking this late? The neighbor's dog started to bark. Bridget mentally retraced her going-to-bed ritual, had she locked all the doors? Confident that she had, she sank down onto her bed.

There it was again. Someone was definitely knocking. Padding silent as a cat in her bare feet, she approached the front door. She let out a sigh, grateful that she had taken the time to slip the safety chain into place. Another quiet knock, this time, more urgent than the last. Bridget pressed her face against the spy hole and switched on the porch light. Daniel's face, nervous and handsome was there, staring straight at the keyhole.

Jerking her face back, Bridget took a moment to decide what to do. What on earth could he want? She imagined he probably wanted to come to beg her to stay quiet about their night together. What a creep! In one swift movement, she had yanked the door open, the safety chain stopping it from opening further than four inches.

"What are you doing here?" She peered at him through the gap with narrowed eyes.

Daniel's smile was sheepish. "Bridget, I was hoping we could talk?"

"What about?"

"Us." He tried to stare seductively through the small gap in the doorway. He looked like an idiot. "I can't forget our night together, can you?" When she said nothing, he continued. "Can I come in? I'm feeling a bit exposed here under the porch light."

Bridget couldn't believe the brazen cheek of the man. "I've got nothing to hide, Daniel, and there isn't any 'us' as you put it." Her words were as sharp as razor blades. "And you've got a bloody cheek coming here and expecting me to be complicit in hurting a beautiful person like Carrie! I'm not in the business of dating married men and even if you don't appreciate your beautiful family, I do. Now rack off, before I call Carrie and tell her everything!" She slammed the door, breathing deeply with anger. Perhaps she should tell Carrie. She didn't deserve to be treated with this kind of callous, disrespect. She deserved to be rid of Daniel. Bridget imagined with satisfaction, Carrie confronting Daniel and kicking him out on the street. But there in the background of her fantasy was a small four-year-old girl crying and a baby who would only ever know weekend visits from his father.

The picture was so sad; she knew that she would never tell. She refused to add to her list of regrets, the destruction of a family.

She didn't hear from Daniel again. In spite of the drama, Bridget felt that Currawong was going to be good for her. It filled her with pride to face her fears, to confront her weaknesses and direct her attention to the needs of others for a while. Carrie was showing her that. Every day, in one way or another, Carrie was doing something to help. It didn't matter if it was a human need or a stray animal, everyone who needed it, got a dose of her kindness and attention. It inspired Bridget to do the same.

The wet season hit Queensland earlier than usual and out of the blue. One afternoon, a couple of weeks after moving in, Bridget sat in her study, staring at the torrential downpour outside. The power was out, there was no TV, and the battery on her laptop was flat and it looked like she would be forced to indulge in a lazy afternoon curled up on the couch with a book. Her phone rang. On the other end, she could hear Carrie over the din of the rain. It sounded like she was inside a tin shed. Carrie was shouting, but Bridget could only catch intermittent words. "Help – deliver shopping – old – car- time?"

Bridget yelled back. "I couldn't really hear what you said, but if you need my help, come and get me. I'll be waiting at my place!" Bridget caught a muffled "Thanks!" and hung up the phone. Fifteen minutes later, she was in the front seat of

Carrie's car in a yellow raincoat. "Okay, what am I helping you with today?"

Carrie grabbed Bridget's hand and squeezed it. "You're an angel for coming. I just need to deliver these meals to some elderly shut-ins today. Their usual delivery service is canceled due to the rain and I couldn't bear it if they went without a meal or a friendly face today. With your help, I'll be able to get it done in half the..." A loud screeching of wheels forced them to turn in terror to their right. A truck had lost control and was sliding from the opposite lane directly into their path. Before the truck slammed into them, Bridget caught a glimpse of the desperate expression on the face of the other driver. And then there was nothing.

She was in the strange house with the corridors again. This time, there was pain. Bridget resisted. She didn't want to have this dream but have it she would. Stretching away into the distance the corridor elongated. The doors came into view, beckoning her to start searching for that elusive something. She tried to grip the walls but her hands slid off, slick and wet. Against her will, she found herself at the first door. I'm running out of time... out of time... Someone was calling her from far away, "Bridget!" they called. I can't find you! She was rummaging through the room, searching. "Bridget!" The voice was louder now, from somewhere nearby, "Please wake up!" She was frantic. Help me find you!

Bridget felt herself emerge from the coma as though traveling an elevator one floor at a time. When she got to the top, her eyes opened. All around her were blurred moving shapes and muffled sounds. Only one shape directly in front of her face stayed still. She focused on it and waited for the blurriness to go away. Gradually, the shape became more distinct, the lines sharper, it was a face. It was Nick's face, wet with tears and he was smiling. Suddenly his face was next to hers and he was sobbing. She didn't know why. But now that Nick was there, everything was going to be all right.

Nick was there every day over the next two weeks in the hospital. Bridget had a concussion, a few broken ribs, a collapsed lung and her spleen had been removed. Nick told her that she had been in a coma for three days after the accident. He had taken the first flight to Queensland and had been by her side ever since. Carrie hadn't fared so well. She was still in a coma in intensive care with multiple broken bones and a head injury.

On her day of discharge, Bridget made her way to Carrie's hospital room. Daniel was by her bedside. His face was white. He looked at Bridget with eyes frantic and bloodshot. She realized in an instant that he was already receiving his punishment, nothing she could say could make him feel worse than he did right now. So, he loved his wife after all; or was this just guilt? Perhaps it was not her place to judge. She took a few ginger steps into the room and gripped the bars at the foot of Carrie's bed.

"How is she?"

Daniel leaned his elbows on the bed and rested his face in his hands. "Not good."

"I think we may have both learned the same lesson from this experience, Daniel. Since I met Carrie I've been judging you for taking your wife for granted. But I now realize that I've been taking someone for granted too, someone who has loved me my whole life and has watched and waited patiently while I've repeatedly thrown myself at people who didn't hold a candle to him. Buddha once said, 'The trouble is; you think you have time,' well now we both know that everything that is important can be taken in an instant. There is no time to waste, we only have now." Bridget turned to go and then hesitating she murmured without looking back. "Take care Daniel, I'll keep you and Carrie in my prayers."

The sunshine was bright in her hospital room when she walked stiffly through the door. Nick had his back to her; he was packing her pajamas and underwear into a duffle bag. Bridget eased her sore body into the chair by the bed and watched him. His big hands were awkward as he fumbled with her silky underwear. His brow was furrowed, his honest, open eyes, tense with the effort, his upturned boyish nose wrinkled in determination. From under her ribs, a wave of peace and security flooded her, filling her up until her heart felt like it would burst. She let out a delighted laugh. Why hadn't she been able to see it before? All the years of pain and misery looking for Mr. Right when she had the perfect man right under her nose the whole time. "I love Nick." Saying it to herself made it all the truer. She loved Nick and when the time was right she would tell him.

"There, he said with finality, zipping up the duffle bag. Where would you like to go next, my lady?"

"Home, please, Nick," she answered, rising to her feet. "Take me home."

LONELY COWBOY

TERI KENDRICK

Frederick spurred his horse onwards through the dwindling autumn sun. He carried a small leather satchel on his person; a satchel that contained all of his belongings. He wasn't a drifter - far from it. He was just a man on the run from his past.

Upon reaching a small town, Frederick cantered his steed through the colourfully painted main street and came to a halt at the side of a tavern. He swung his leg over the horse's saddle and leapt to the floor, swinging his satchel from his shoulder to reach for a frayed rope within it. Using the rope, he tied his horse to a wooden beam, and walked towards the saloon's set of swinging doors, his boots thumping heavily against the splintered wooden decking. He pushed open the door and made his way inside. It was a noisy room, filled with chatter and cigar smoke.

Frederick walked directly to the bar and perched himself on one of the tall wooden pedestals that overlooked the rows of spirits and brews behind the counter. The bartender, a young man with dark brown eyes and fair hair, greeted him with a friendly smile. "What can I do you for?" He spoke with a warm tone. "A serving of your finest brew, and a room too, if there's one free." Frederick dropped a pile of crumpled dollar notes on the counter, and the waiter nodded, sliding a drink across the counter towards him.

Frederick nursed the sweet cider as he took in his surroundings. He noticed a group of suited men playing blackjack at a table, a drunken argument between two drunks, and finally, a beautiful young red-haired girl, whom was playing a quiet, yet soulful melody on the piano that was nestled in a corner away from the tables. There was something very alluring about her; her ruby hair danced onto her shoulders in light locks, and her sapphire eyes gazed peacefully out from her sweeping fringe. He caught himself looking for a little too long, and turned back towards the bar.

Frederick sipped more of the liquid from the brim of the glass and let it line his throat with a warm sensation before ordering another. He set it down upon the counter before turning back towards the piano, but the young girl who had caught his attention was now gone. He caught the bartender's attention and ordered another drink.

Setting another empty glass upon the top, Frederick peered around the room once more. By this time, a glimmering glow radiating from a chandelier of candles replaced the sunlight, which had turned into a dark, foggy night. Frederick retired to his room, his footsteps thudding against the wooden floor as he navigated the maze of tables, making his way to the stairs. He climbed up towards the landing, and headed towards the door at the end of the hall, twisting they key that he had been given in the barrel of the lock. The door pushed open with a creak, and he made his way into the room.

Inside, the smell of burned candle wax filled the room. It wasn't a luxury room by any means, but it would do while he was laying low – a small room in a small, quiet town. It was plain yet cosy, and it had been kept minimal – the bed was positioned in the centre with a locker at its food, and a small oak rocking-chair looked out of the window. Aside from a frosted glass mirror that hung from the wall, these were the only furnishings in the room.

Frederick placed his belongings carefully in the footlocker before sliding on top of the bed, nodding away into a sleep with ease, thanks to the help of his consumption of cider.

Frederick awoke the next morning to the dazzling sunlight burning into the room, his eyes taking a few moments to adjust as he opened them slowly. Sitting up on the bed, he reached into the footlocker for his satchel and emptied the remainder of his money onto the bed's mattress, spreading it out with his hands as he counted it. He didn't have much, but it would last him until he'd found some work. He'd paid enough cash to rent the room for the next few weeks, so he had shelter, and food... Well, he was a capable hunter, so he didn't have to worry about that. The money would probably be spent on alcohol, anyway.

He draped his linen shirt over his body and hoisted his faded denim jeans up to his waist before peering into to the mirror, reaching into his satchel again for his comb. He styled his brunette hair neatly with a parting to the side before he stroked his burly facial hair. Taking a seat on the rocking-chair, he peered out through the thin netted curtains and admired what the town had to offer.

In the way of shops, there was a general store opposite the tavern, and hunting shop a few buildings down, as well as a handful of street merchants who had set up shop in the middle of the dirt road. Beyond the rows of rooftops, he could see that the town was beginning to become a part of the steam revolution; builders worked frantically through the heat to lay down tracks. He glanced towards them – perhaps he would look at getting work with them. Not *yet,* though. He still needed to let his past fade away a little. First, he would take a few easy days to acquaint himself with his new surroundings.

Frederick made his way down into the bar of the now-empty saloon. It was a far cry from the bustle of the bar in the evening; the air was clean, and without a thick smog brewing from the tips of cigars, the wooden chairs were arranged neatly around tables, and the staff navigated the room in a calm, orderly fashion. The barman nodded politely at Frederick as he made his way out of the door, and Frederick returned the gesture.

Deciding to take a look around the shops, he made his way to the general store after tending to his horse and taking it to the stables on the other side of town. In fact, there were a few useful items in there which he scooped into his arms and carried to the front desk. Waiting for the clerk after he had rung the bell, he heard a soft, comforting female voice coming from the corridor behind the building's shop area. Upon hearing the content of the words, however, Frederick listened with concern.

"It's okay, Father," Came the voice, "I'm sure the stock delivery will come soon – they probably had to go a longer way around where they're working on the railway construction. Please, please please don't panic. You can't afford to get stressed with your condition as it is."

A hoarse, rasping voice soon followed, "Don't you see, Theresa? I need this stock to come in. If we have no stock to shift, how will we make money? If I can't afford my medicine... then who knows what might happen."

There was a scurrying of footsteps in the corridor, and Frederick glanced down at his satchel as he counted the money to pay for his goods.

"I'm sorry to keep you waiting, Sir." The came voice again, dancing into his ears sweetly.

"It's fine," Frederick smiled as he looked back up towards the source of the voice.

Upon seeing the girl's elegant facial features, Frederick froze on the spot, almost speechless at her beauty – it was the red-haired girl that had caught his fancy at the saloon the previous night.

Her skin was soft and glimmered gorgeously in the natural light that filtered through the panelled windows, and despite her obviously going through difficult times, she wore a brave, attractive smile upon her skin.

After paying, Frederick turned to leave the shop but paused in his steps. He hesitated for a few moments before swinging on the balls of his feet to turn Theresa again.

"You know," he began to speak, "I'm not gonna pretend that I didn't hear the conversation that happened back there. To me, that really didn't sound good. Look, I'm a... err... traveller and I know first hand that it's a rough place out there in the open expanse of the desert. Any number of things could have happened to your stock delivery. Besides, winter is coming. This could be the last large delivery you can get for the season."

Theresa sighed before releasing the half-forced smile from her cheeks.

"I know, I know." She broke her voice into a whisper before adding, "But my father. He's ill; I want to at least be able to give him some hope."

"How about you tell me where it was supposed to be coming from?" he suggested, "I'll ride out this morning and see if I can find any trace of it."

"You'd... do that? For a stranger?" Asked Theresa with a shocked but grateful tone in her voice.

"Well," joked Frederick, "I'd like someone to help me like this someday; that's for sure. Let's just hope that karma works out as it should."

Truthfully, Frederick had ulterior motives at play; Theresa was a stunning woman, and he knew that there weren't many girls with as much natural beauty as her around. He knew that should she accept his offer, he'd at least have another chance at hearing her soothing voice once more, even if his mission should not prove successfully.

"I can't do that," sighed Theresa, "I can't put someone in danger just for a wagon of stock."

"Seriously, I insist," Frederick said firmly and reassuringly, "After-all, it would be your Father you'd be putting in danger if you didn't let me do this."

Theresa stayed on the spot for a few seconds before she nodded her head silently, reluctantly agreeing to his help.

"Thank you," she smiled softly, "I won't forget this."

Frederick swiftly turned away from the shop after Theresa had given him the details of the wagon, and he hurried briskly to the stables where he had left his horse.

He leaped onto the horse's back and spurred it onwards, steering it out of the paddock as its mighty hooves pounded against the worn dirt path below.

The sky was clear, leaving the sun to kiss Frederick's back as he followed the pathway away from town, riding into an embankment between two red-rock cliff-faces by the side of the path.

The route was desolate aside from the occasional rattle of a snake, or call of a bird as it swooped gracefully over his head, and as the rock banks by the side of the paths became taller, he began to ride into the valley's shadow before reaching a crossroad.

Supposedly, the wagon was coming from the town towards the east, so Frederick followed that path. He rode for a while before coming to a rickety bridge that towered over a ravine. He came to a halt and jumped off his horse, anchoring his feet into the ground as he landed. He inspected the site; if he was a highwayman, this would be the perfect location to hi-jack a wagon – there was a ledge just beneath the bridge where he could easily hide, and no-one would be able to see him for miles.

Frederick jumped onto the ledge and crouched next to the sand – someone had been here recently; there were still fresh footprints in the dirt. He jumped back onto the footpath and carefully followed the feint trail of a set of wheels that veered away from the path as he attempted to track down a wagon that may or may not be the one that he was watching out for.

He jumped onto the back of his horse and followed the trail for a mile or so before the trail disappeared behind the face of a rock and into a dark enclosure between several walls of stone.

Silently and cautiously, he dismounted the horse again and crept through the shadows until he reached a small bandit camp. There was the wagon – right in the centre of several canvas tents. The bandits appeared to be sleeping, so he edged towards the wagon, a sense of adrenaline beginning to pulse vigorously through his veins, his right hand hovering over the holster of his pistol as he carefully trod through the camp.

Reaching the wagon, he pulled himself up onto the wooden step, a bead of sweat forming on his eyebrow as its wooden platform creaked beneath him. He paused and peered around the camp before he continued. An empty sack lay conveniently at the foot of a pile of goods, which he picked up and stowed quietly in the bag. He swung it over his shoulder and made his way back toward his horse. That was, until he noticed a hog-tied victim staring at him in urgency for rescue in one of the tents, presumably the driver of the wagon.

Frederick couldn't just leave the man here, so instead, he set the sack down before he approached him. His nose was bloody, and his shirt had crimson stains on it. The men had hurt him bad. Frederick crouched down before him and rummaged through the contents of his bags before his palms came to a rest on the leather grip of his hunting blade. He brandished it and began to saw through the thick rope that bound the man's wrists and feet together.

Eventually, the rope came free of him and his body thumped with relief against he hard floor. He immediately rose to his feet, ready to follow Frederick to safety. He grabbed the sack and lead the man silently towards the horse.

"Get on," Frederick whispered urgently, "We need to get out of here."

The two men rode on the back of the horse, kicking up a cloud of dust behind them as they hurried back to the safety of the town.

"I owe you my life," Breathed the man heavily, "I'm forever in your debt. Please... just let me know what I can do... anything... to pay you back."

Frederick tilted his head to face the man. "You know, there might just be something. You see, the girl that runs the store, her Father has seen better days and they need every penny they can get to pay off the bills for his medicines. I'd really appreciate you letting them off the costs of this shipment." He patted the sack that was slung over his shoulders as he spoke.

"Theresa's old man is ill? Why didn't she just say so? Look, anything to help, it will be the last shipment I can offer them anyway. With no wagon anymore, it looks like I'm gonna be out of business for a while anyway. Hopefully it can tide them over until they find a new trader"

The horse pulled up outside Theresa's, and Frederick secured it after sliding off the saddle. He wandered coolly into the store with the sack slung over his shoulder, and Alex, the trader, following in his wake. He marched triumphantly towards the front desk and placed the sack down. Theresa's younger sister clung to her sides. She could barely be 5 years old – she probably had no clue what was going on, the poor girl.

Theresa smiled thankfully as she peered into the sack and approached Frederick. Her lips grazed lightly against Frederick's cheek as she kissed his skin lightly in thanks, sending a chilled feeling reverberating through his spine. For those few short moments, he was in a sense of bliss.

"Oh Alex, what have they done to you!?" She gasped upon realizing his bloodied shirt. She drew away from Frederick and hurried towards Alex, wrapping him securely in her arms after she had She turned to her sister, and ushered her through into the living quarters.

In an instant, the feeling of bliss turned into one of jealousy as he watched her cradle him. Was it wrong to feel this way about someone he first spoke to this morning? Maybe. But Frederick's grandma had once told him; "When it comes to love, always trust your heart. It is the one thing that knows what one truly desires." And his heart was telling him that he desired Theresa.

"Come," whispered Theresa sympathetically to Alex, "Come get changed – you can borrow an outfit of my father's. I'm sure he won't mind, given the circumstances." Alex followed her and emerged a few minutes later wearing a set of baggy trousers and a fresh shirt.

Alex broke the news that he would no longer be able to trade with them, leaving Theresa in a state of worry and panic; sure, they were now fully stocked – but how long would it be before they were running low on supplies once again? What would happen if they couldn't find a new merchant on time? The results could be catastrophic – supplies were scarce enough as it was, and finding a trustworthy, honest supplier like Alex was a rare occurrence in this day and age.

Frederick leaned against a shelf and observed Theresa. He could see her worries, and wanted to ease her worries away. He piped up, "What if I helped you gather supplies for a while? Just until you can find a new supplier. Sure, I won't be able to source quite as much as an experienced trader could, but at least I could keep things on your shelves."

"Frederick, you've already done so much for us – how could I expect you to do anything more? It's not fair."

"Then let's make it fair – in exchange, I won't ask much. Just for cooked food in my stomach and your company."

Alex cut into the conversation, "Well, I'll leave you love-birds to your chatter. I'm not sure that I need to hear where this conversation is going – you'll be able to find me in the saloon if you need me." he made his way out of the building and across the street, leaving Frederick and Theresa alone in the store.

Almost in an instant, Theresa began to advance towards Frederick. She began to lower her eyelids as she moved within touching distance of him, tilting her head backwards as she traced her palm down his back. Their lips began to graze against one another, but they were interrupted by a deep groaning coming from the halls beyond the shop. Theresa separated herself from Frederick's gentle touch and dashed into the hallway urgently to tend to her father.

Not wanting to intrude her fathers privacy, Frederick waited in the shop. A short while later, Theresa emerged from the door-frame that separated the shop from her home with a concerned expression spread across the soft skin of her face. "I'm sorry about that," She sighed, "His condition is getting worse. He can barely even move without putting himself through pain." Frederick tried his best to comfort her; he could see that she was a fragile character and that her father's situation was worrying for her, so he consoled her as a single tear began to roll down her cheeks. Through a break in her tears, she began to breathe heavily before whispering into Frederick's ear softly. "Thank you, thank you for everything you're doing for me. I don't think I could handle this situation on my own."

"I'd like to introduce you to my father - it pains me to say it, though I don't think he's got long left. I think he'd really appreciate Meeting a kind gentleman like you." Frederick agreed and followed Theresa through into the home. It was well maintained, and the sweet scent of flowers flowed through the house. Frederick admired her; not only was she taking care of her father and her sister, but her home was immaculately presented, as was the store - she must have worked solidly with no spare time.

They entered through a polished wooden door on the right side of the corridor. A slight breeze pushed the curtains aside from the open window, and a bouquet of flowers were arranged by the bedside. "Father, this is Frederick. He's helping with the store." The man's fragile body turned slowly in the bed as he turned to face Frederick. His skin was pale, and a thin layer of sweat made his skin glisten in the light. Despite his condition though, he seemed to be keeping relatively cheerful. He smiled welcomingly towards Frederick and slowly offered his hand in greeting, which Frederick shook lightly. Theresa left the room and strolled towards the kitchen to prepare dinner. She invited Frederick into the living room, but her father insisted that he stay.

Frederick chose to sit by the man's bedside, and the two of them made eye contact, before her father began to speak in a raspy voice. "You seem like a good man Frederick. I'm glad that my daughter has been lucky enough to meet a good person like you." "Thank you," whispered Frederick, tilting his head towards to old man. "Listen. My days are numbered. That's no secret," he began to talk in a quiet voice so that Theresa couldn't hear, "I want you to promise me something." "What would you have me promise?" asked Frederick in response. Theresa's father paused for a few seconds as her footsteps clicked through the hallway when she tended to a customer in the shop. After she was gone, he began to speak again. "Theresa... she pretends to be stronger than she is. When I'm gone, she'll need someone that can help her stand up strong. I'd like you to take care of her Frederick. Would you grant that wish for an old man?"

Frederick didn't even need to hesitate before he answered confidently. "Yes. Yes, I'll do that." He smiled at Frederick as he answered, with a comforting sense of security flowing through his body. The scent of smoked hog began to waft pleasantly through the house before Theresa peered into the bedroom where the Men were deep in conversation. She balanced one of the clay plates on her arm, offering it to her father. "No, I'll come through and sit at the table. Please, I insist. We have a guest, it would be rude not to." Theresa supported her father as he rose to his feet and walked weakly across the hallway, dragging his feet against the mahogany floorboards as he walked.

He slumped into the chair and gazed peacefully at his daughter, who was now wearing a smile upon her face; her smile was the reason that he had managed to stay in relatively high spirits. "I see the way that you smile at him, Theresa. I see the way that he smiles at you too." Her father observed. Theresa's cheeks began to paint themselves a bright scarlet as she blushed, and immediately, her father began to joke at her expense, in a cheerful and playful tone.

" You've gone as red as a tomato!" Her sister remarked. Her father laughed before coughing heavily into his hands. "Make sure this one doesn't get away, oh daughter of mine." Frederick chuckled and peered up at Theresa, whom was still blushing. "I apologise on behalf of my father," Theresa giggled, "He just gets worse with age!"

The day rolled into night, and Frederick became rather well acquainted with the family, sharing several stories around the dinner table as his knife sliced into the tender, succulent meat. He came to realize just how poor their situation was – the family were just managing to get by. The profits of the general store were the only thing keeping a roof over their heads and food on their plates.

Should their stock become any more scarce, then they may not have a home any longer. Frederick vowed that he would do his best to keep merchandise on the shelves once again, and he could tell that his promise meant a lot to the family.

Eventually, Frederick strolled across the street and back to his room at the saloon, laying on his back atop the soft mattress of the bed. He stared at the ceiling, deep in thought. He couldn't get Theresa away from his mind – her soft, beautiful face seemed to float gracefully at the forefront of his mind, and her gentle voice reverberated softly in his daydream. He eventually drifted into a slumber after laying awake for a short while.

The days turned into weeks, and Frederick began his task of sourcing goods, riding his horse into the far corners of the state in order to keep Theresa's store profitable. It was a little bit different to the kind of jobs he was used to doing, but it was... good. The air breezed over his cheeks as he encouraged his horse to gallop, and though time consuming, it was relatively easy. Most of all, though, he enjoyed the sight of Theresa's gorgeous smile upon his return to the store.

One evening, though, the smile had been replaced by a flurry of tears as she crouched on the porch step that lead into the store. Immediately, Frederick feared for the worst. He leapt from his horse and his heels pounded against the floor, leaving a cloud of dust in his wake as he dashed towards her.

She looked at him, and choked on her sobs as she tried to force out a sentence.

"It's father... he's... he's gone. He passed in his sleep."

Frederick sat next to her, trying to fight back a tear that began to roll down his own cheek; her father was a good, honest man, and even in the short time that he had known the three of them, they had begun to feel like family. Theresa tucked her head onto his chest, and her tears shimmered in the sunlight as they rolled onto Frederick's shirt. The two of them sat there for what felt like an eternity, until the banks of Theresa's eyes had leaked all of their tears.

The two of them attended the burial, and Theresa gripped Frederick's hand tightly throughout the ceremony as the coffin was lowered into its resting place. Theresa peered around at the group that had gathered and smiled proudly as she began to realize just how much her father meant to the people of the town. A large crowd mourned his passing, and throughout the day, many bouquets of flowers were left on the shop's rough wooden porch.

As the sun began to set over the mountains in the distance, a peaceful night sky began to pass over the town. Slowly, Theresa began to accept the fact that her father was now in a better place, free of his pain. Frederick and Theresa began to stroll into the wilderness away from the town before they found a soft sandy mound which they lay on, gazing up into the colourfully painted sky. After a short while, a single star began to appear. Theresa pointed up towards it before she whispered into Frederick's ear.

"You see that star? That's going to be my Daddy's star."

"It's a beautiful star," responded Frederick, "A very deserving one to be called your father's."

Theresa snuggled into Frederick's grip and gazed at him lovingly. He wasn't like the others. He was loving, understanding, and patient. He was here to stay – she hoped, anyway.

Frederick ran his fingers through her ruby locks and returned her gaze before their lips met.

This time, there were no distractions. It was just them, and the never ending sea of colours that were painted in the heavens by a glorious sunset.

Their lips wrapped around one another as they enjoyed a loving embrace, and Frederick trailed his fingers over the delicate skin of her cheeks as her mouth's sweet taste rolled onto his tongue.

After they had shown their affection for one another, Theresa rested her head on his chest once again, the two of them peacefully watching the stars begin to flicker in the dark night sky. They eventually rose to their feet and returned home, Theresa slipping her palm into his as they walked.

Frederick was kept busy over the coming weeks, with a surge of customers coming in to pay their respects to Theresa's father. There seemed to be an increased demand for their goods, meaning that he spent most of his days riding out to nearby ranches to haggle over the prices of their products. Without the costs of her father's medicines, the store began to spin a healthy profit, and as she came to terms with her father's passing, Frederick noticed that a healthy natural shine began to envelop her skin, and a natural smile became a permanent fixture on her face.

With the profits, Theresa began to decorate the shop with marvellous decorations, giving the small, cosy shop an illusion of grandeur. It fast became one of the town's landmarks due to Frederick's helping hand, and they became well respected members of the community.

Frederick returned home one evening, leaving his horse at the stables. He stroked its fine mane and patted its back before he began to stroll through the town's main-street. He saw many familiar faces, most of which nodded their head in greeting, which he returned.

His footsteps thumped onto the wooden porch and then into the store. He flung his satchel from his back and removed his daily haul of merchandise, which he set carefully onto the shelves. Theresa appeared through the door-frame as Frederick admired the work which they had accomplished over the last few months.

"Your shop looks great, Theresa!" He smiled proudly.

"It's not my shop," she whispered in response, "It's *our* shop."

They stared lovingly into one another's eyes for a few seconds before their eyelids drew to a close in harmony, their lips grazing as they stood in the warmth of a romantic embrace. Frederick smiled with the corner of his mouth. He had every intention of keeping the promise that he had made to her father. It was an exciting new start; he finally felt like he was free – perhaps he would even be able to begin a family of his own.

REDEEMABLE

RICKI CROSS

<u>Upstate</u>

He knew what it was before the courier got out of the van. Even the neighbors peering from their windows like buzzards for the carcass could detect the scent of complete annihilation. As the heavyset messenger lumbered up the snow-lined driveway and met him on the front steps, Patrick felt the sick sensation of defeat in his stomach and without a word, held out his hand to accept the manila envelope the man in the khaki uniform was handing him.

"Are you Reverend Patrick Dean?" the carrier asked. Swallowing the lump in his throat, Patrick nodded. "I need you to sign this, Mr. Dean. You've been served."

Without argument, Patrick took the pen and scribbled his name before retreating quickly into the house with the package before the tears flowed from his burning eyes. He leaned heavily against the door and exhaled slowly, trying to collect himself. Then, he moved to the staircase and sat down. With trembling hands, he tore open the envelope and read the dreaded contents. Cynthia had filed for a divorce. A divorce. The word reverberated through his skull like a bullet. Of course he had been expecting it but the reality was still almost too much for him to stomach.

Unsteadily, he rose to his feet. He tried to remember the last time he had eaten. He couldn't recall his last meal. That was probably a bad sign. He wiped his tired, streaked eyes and walked into the kitchen, determined to reclaim some of his former strength. His life may have been falling apart but he was still a strong man, a man of God and God would want him to live and fight another day. *God wouldn't want you divorcing your wife,* a snide voice in his ear whispered. Patrick shoved the thought out of his head and yanked open the fridge with too much force. A glass ketchup bottle fell to the floor and shattered. Jamba came running eagerly into the room, smelling food like the little scavenger she was.

"No! Get out of here before you cut your paw!" he commanded the bloodhound. She paused uncertainly and slowly backed away, giving him a hurt look. As he quickly cleaned up the mess, he realized that the ketchup he had just disposed of was just about the last staple of food left in his refrigerator. A scan of the pantry produced the same results. He needed to go shopping. He had been to the grocery store once since Cynthia had left almost three weeks prior. Shuffling into the hall, he ushered Jamba up the stairs and changed out of his robe into a pair of raggedy track pants and old sweatshirt. The dog looked up at him expectantly, her tail wagging. Patrick was overcome by guilt. When was the last time he had taken the pooch on a decent walk? He vowed he would do that when he got back from the store. He scratched her ears affectionately and grabbed his keys off the dresser, purposely avoiding the reflection in the mirror. He knew what it would show; a man riddled with shame and anguish.

Thankfully the snow had stopped falling during the night and only the white mounds piled on the side of the road were reminiscent of the two-day storm that had finally ended. As Patrick pulled into the small parking lot of the local grocer, he was relieved to find it almost deserted. It was a Tuesday morning after all. Hurriedly, he slipped inside and pulled a cart into the produce section. Without much regard for what he was selecting, he began throwing items in, hoping to be in and out before the inevitable occurred. Yet, as he rounded the corner into the condiment aisle, he almost collided with a young boy who was crouched near the floor, peering at the pickles with intense scrutiny. The child looked up at him, startled and then his serious expression melted into a huge smile.

"Pastor Pat!" he yelled. Patrick cringed, feeling the blood drain from his face. The boy ran over and threw his arms around the older man. Patrick gently hugged young Austin back and released him, looking around for his mother. As if on cue, she came storming up the lane and seized her son's hand, glaring viciously at Patrick.

"Pastor Pat where have you been? We keep looking for you at church but you don't go up on stage and talk anymore!"

"No, Austin, I don't do sermons at the church anymore," Patrick said quietly, averting his eyes from the woman's steely gaze.

"Oh! Why not? I like it when you tell the stories about the animals and the boat and the snake and the giant. The other Pastor is no fun. He just reads pages out of this big boring book." If Patrick hadn't been so depressed, he would have chuckled at the five-year old's interpretations.

"You should give Pastor Michael a chance, Austin. He is a very nice man," Patrick chided, chucking the child under his chin.

"More importantly, son, he is not a drunk, an adulterer or a sinner," Austin's mother chimed, pulling her son from Patrick's reach. Both Austin and Patrick blinked at her tone. Patrick's face turned crimson and as he excused himself, he heard Austin say, "Mom, what's a dalter?"

Somehow, Patrick managed to purchase the few objects he had tossed into the cart and make it home in a fog. When Jamba greeting him at the door, he completely forsook his promise to take her for a walk and after haphazardly throwing the groceries into the kitchen, he threw himself onto his bed and stared hopelessly up at the ceiling. *I am a pariah. This will haunt me for the rest of my life. I need to get out of here.* There was something cold and wet on his hand. Jamba had followed him into the room and was nuzzling his hand with a cold nose. He petted her head absently and as he sat up, his eyes fell onto a worn photograph on the dresser. Slowly, he rose to his feet and picked up the picture. While the frame had been there for as long as he could remember, he hadn't heeded its existence in years. Gently, he wiped the dust off the silver and smiled wistfully at his own happy expression in the image. He had been so young, holding a fishing pole and grinning without a care in the world. But it was the property in the background which held his attention. Patrick knew where he had to go.

<u>Down South</u>

It was just as dirty and dilapidated as he remembered. There were even more holes in the roof than the last time he had visited and at least one hurricane had eaten away at most of the siding. Thankfully, the cabin was miniscule enough that the contractor with whom he had spoken guaranteed a full repair in about a week but until then, Patrick and Jamba were going to be contending with the elements.

As man and dog slowly ascended the rickety steps, under the humble cypress trees, some feral animal mewled angrily and hissed from under the slats in the porch. Jamba yelped in fear but Patrick was overwhelmed with nostalgia of childhood. This cottage had been in his family for four generations. His great grandparents had built it and birthed all twelve of their children within its five rooms. His father had been born there, along with six of his aunts. After that era, the place had been used strictly as a getaway property for the cousins but as everyone aged and became successful, the majority of the family had left the deep south and ventured onto "better" things. Suddenly everyone had cabins in Aspen or summer homes in the Hamptons. It seemed that Patrick was apparently to only one who felt a kinship to the rundown house, despite its sorry state. Granted, he didn't spend the time he wanted in the bayou but he had always had a great affection for the property and its history.

The door was not locked and Patrick rolled his suitcase into the tiny front room which was both the kitchen and living room. Grandpa's antique rocker was still there and while there were spider webs in every corner, the potbelly stove was where he remembered, the tiny bar fridge was in the kitchen and even the wash basin was by the back door. *If this were the city, there would be nothing left. Someone would have stolen all the belongings and some squatters would be living in attic.* But this was not the city. This was the serene, trusting south where things were still sacred and people watched out for one another. He reached out and flicked a light switch but of course there was no electricity. He would have to tend to that tomorrow. Beside him, Jamba whined again. She was out of her element but the truth was, the reason Patrick had rescued her from the shelter was that she reminded him of one of his grandpa's hunting hounds. He had even named her Jamba for Jambalaya despite Cynthia's protests.

"What an awful name for a dog! It's bad enough that she's so ugly! Take her back and get something smaller and cuter, Pat!" Yet the dog had stuck and so had the name and it had truly been the only reminder Patrick had of his childhood in the womb of America. From under the rocker, a scared green snake slithered out and disappeared into a crack in the slat floor. Jamba howled and ran out of the still open screen door.

"Jamba!" Patrick dropped his suitcase and tore after her down the dirt road. He caught glimpse of her tail disappear around the corner and he rushed toward the bushes. Panting, he turned around the bend and stopped abruptly. Jamba was in the arms of a boy of maybe eight, shivering in fright. But behind the child and dog was a woman standing in the doorway of her cottage. Patrick could make out the tall outline of a black haired woman in a blue dress but he could not see her face. Even so, she took his breath away – or at least the little breath he had left after chasing his hound.

"Jamba! Come!" Patrick found his voice. Reluctantly, the dog slunk out of the boy's lap and retreated to his master. The woman stepped out of the home and Patrick's heart leapt into his throat as the beauty of her face enthralled him. She had big blue eyes filled with wisdom and compassion, a lovely cream complexion and a welcoming smile.

"I'm so sorry! She got frightened off by a snake. She's never seen one before," Patrick heard himself babble. The woman's smile widened.

"Well I understand that," she replied with a sweet Southern drawl which only enhanced her attractiveness. "She ain't hurting nobody ova here. Damien 'n I love dogs, don't we, honey?"

The young boy nodded eagerly, dark eyes wide but his lips did not move. The woman continued forward. She wiped her hands on the apron covering the skirt of her dress and offered a palm to Patrick. He accepted it and noticed how soft were her hands.

"Sarah Jane," she said. "An' this is ma son, Damien. Y'all ain't from around here. I kin tell."

Patrick shook his head.

"I'm Patrick. This is Jamba. We're from...out of town." Patrick was reluctant to give her too much information. The idea was to retreat from people, not make new friends to disappoint.

"We jus' moved here from Baton Rouge 'bout a year ago. Where y'all stayin'?" Patrick pointed down the road.

"In the Dean's place. It's my family's but no one much uses it anymore." Sarah Jane raised an eyebrow in surprise.

"Y'all can't stay there! All them 'coons and cats be livin' up in there now. It ain't safe nor sanitary!"

"I have contractors coming to fix it up. We won't be like this too long," Patrick assured her. He suddenly noticed Damien staring intently at him.

"How old are you, Damien?" Patrick asked. He had always liked children and they seemed to feel the same about him. The boy did not answer but he did not look away.

"Damien don't talk much," Sarah Jane said quietly. Patrick nodded understandingly. He smiled at the boy.

"Nothing wrong with that," he replied. "Still waters always run the deepest."

A look of surprise and appreciation flashed through Sarah Jane's lovely eyes.

"Why don't y'all get settled in and come back fer dinner. Y'all like gumbo? Ma pa always said I make the best gumbo this side of New Orleans."

"If it's all right with your husband. I wouldn't want to impose." Patrick almost choked on the word "husband." He had no idea what had come over him. He never had attractions like this to perfect strangers but for some reason he was drawn to this woman. *You need to walk away before you get yourself in even more trouble,* he warned himself. But his own warning went unheeded. Sarah Jane laughed throatily.

"If y'all kin find him, y'all kin ask him yourself," she chuckled. "We ain't seen Damien's pa since the boy was knee high to a grasshopper." Patrick wasn't sure if he was contrite or relieved. Probably a bit of both. "Y'all come at 6. Bring yer Jamba. I'll have a bowl fer her too."

Back at the shack, Patrick perched gently on his grandpa's rocker and began to sway back and forth. He was thinking about Sarah Jane and the sense that he had known her for a long while. He wondered if her black waves were as soft as they appeared. Guiltily, he tried to shift his thoughts but he couldn't seem to get her smile out of his head with the slight gap between her teeth and the endearing but almost inaudible lisp her mouth produced. Her eyes reminded him of someone...abruptly, Patrick sat up in the wooden chair, startling Jamba from her sleeping position at his feet. Shame stained his cheeks a scarlet he feared would never fade. He realized exactly why he found Sarah Jane so desirable; she was a physical combination of his wife and the woman with whom he had ruined the sanctity of his marriage.

Upstate
One Month Prior

"I really have no interest in going, Cyndi," Patrick sighed as he finished tying his tie in the full length mirror. "I don't see why I need to be there."

"Oh Pat, you're marrying them next week. Just go, have a scotch, make a toast and come home. It's your duty to attend these events." Patrick sighed again and turned to face his wife, feeling a slight sense of jealousy. She was already in her pajamas, curled up in bed with her knitting. He knew she was right. Bachelor parties were a rite of passage and he was hosting the ceremony for the happy couple but he had never been a fan of the ritual. He was always secretly relieved when the grooms planned rowdy

gatherings and opted to leave him out of them. He would much rather be home playing ball with Jamba or reading a book.

Dutifully, he dropped a kiss on Cynthia's cheek and headed out of the bedroom.

"Please don't forget to let Jamba out before you go to bed."

"You don't need to remind me every time you leave the house, Pat. I'll let her out." Patrick paused at the doorway and looked back at his other half. She was still a lovely woman, even after fifteen years of marriage. Her honey blonde hair was always well coifed, her nails perfectly manicured and she had vivid, intelligent blue eyes which he had initially fallen in love with what seemed like a million years ago. Even ready for bed, she had a cold cream mask on her face and curlers in her hair in preparation for tomorrow.

"Cynthia, please don't neglect Jamba. She is getting older and her bladder can't handle holding it for long periods of time." Cynthia dropped the scarf she was working on and glared at him.

"Are you suggesting that I don't take care of your stupid dog? I always let her out, Patrick!"

Patrick held his ground.

"Last week when I came home from my conference, she had peed on the welcome rug. She never does anything like that unless she hasn't been out. I'm just asking you to remember, that's all." Cynthia sat forward rigidly in the bed, incensed.

"Well maybe something's wrong with her because I'm always letting her out when you're away. And if you don't trust me to do it, then hire someone to do it for you, you ungrateful boor! I take darn good care of that useless animal even though I didn't want her. But you didn't seem to care and brought her home anyway. Now I'm not babysitting properly for you. You are insufferable, Patrick. You better go before I say something I regret." Biting his lip, Patrick heeded her advice and left the house, fuming.

He was at the venue housing the bachelor party in fifteen minutes. The groomsmen had chosen a quaint lakeside tavern for the party. It promised *to be low key and well behaved but Patrick was still shaking with anger when he walked inside. He tried to stuff his emotions under a superficial smile and greeted the other party goers. But he couldn't get to the bar fast enough where he ordered his first scotch.*

Two hours had gone by and Patrick had really no recount of where the time had escaped but around ten thirty p.m. he was chatting to a mysterious sloe eyed beauty in a dimly lit corner of the restaurant. Her luxuriant black hair caught the candlelight like magic flecks and while later Patrick could not recall what they had discussed, he remembered wanting to hear her speak so he could listen to her mellifluous, throaty voice. An hour later, the groom had approached him to gently question how he was getting home and Patrick was apparently sitting very close to the ethereal beauty in the booth, still drinking scotch (at least he was told the following day).

By this point he had turned off his phone to avoid Cynthia's texts and phone calls.

Midnight found Patrick with the exotic stranger in the bathroom in a very compromising position. Two of the groomsmen had walked in on the act and quickly exited, waiting for Patrick to come out of the washroom so they could drive him home. He was barely coherent from the amount of alcohol he had consumed. They quietly unlocked his front door and gently pushed him into the house, awkwardly dressed and falling down. Neither of the men had wanted to explain to Mrs. Dean how her husband had come to be in such a state or be forced to answer any questions. The only certainty Patrick had at that point was that Jamba had not been let out for she urinated all over his feet as soon as he stumbled into the house.

The following morning, the entire town's phone lines were afire. It was too juicy a scandal to ignore. Pastor Pat was drunk and cheating on his wife with a stranger in front of members of his own parish? He was an instant outcast. He didn't even have time to beg Cynthia for forgiveness. By the time he had slept off the alcohol, he was staring at her emptied closet and dresser drawers.

Down South

Patrick snapped out of his reverie of mortification and glanced at his watch. Sarah Jane would be expecting him and Jamba very shortly.

"Come on, girl," he said to the pooch and they hurried out of the cottage down the road. As they neared the bushes, Patrick heard screaming. He and Jamba paused mid-step and listened. The shrieking continued from Sarah Jane's house. He began to run toward the commotion. Tearing around the corner, there was a crash and Damien threw open the screen and took off like the devil himself was on his heels. Tears streaked his face and he was wailing high and feral but he had disappeared before Patrick could react. When he looked back at the house, Sarah Jane stood on the threshold looking defeated. She tried to force a smile as she saw him but failed. Tears misted her incredible eyes as she waved for them to enter.

"I'm sorry y'all had to see that," she said, tiredly as she shooed them into her small home. "Damien has good days and bad ones. This ain't been the best one."

"We can do this another day. Please go deal with your son," Patrick said, gently. Sarah Jane shook her head.

"Oh no! I been slavin' away over a hot stove all day. Y'all gonna stay and eat. Damien will be back when he calms down some. Dontcha worry. It happens all the time. It's one of the reasons I decided to move all the way out ta here. Ain't no one to witness his breakdowns. In Baton Rouge, ma neighbors done be callin' the police an' Child Services on me once a week. No one understands what it's like." Her normally bright eyes were clouded with sadness.

"If you don't mind me asking, have you taken him to a doctor?"

Sarah Jane gestured for him to sit down at a modest kitchen table done in solid pine. She laughed mirthlessly.

"Yessir. An' all of them want to put him on this drug an' that drug. I even had him try some of them. Turned him into a zombie or robot or somethin'. Ain't no way for a child to live. So I keep him home an' school him here but I ain't the most educated woman but when I think of the alternative, I might as well lock him up in an asylum." She choked on her last words and sobbed. Her hand flew to her mouth as she tried to stifle the raw emotion she was feeling. Patrick was instantly at her side, embracing her. She stiffened at his unexpected touch and he backed away immediately.

"Oh, I'm so sorry! I didn't mean to – "

"No no! It ain't you, Patrick. It's...I ain't really had much male companionship since Damien's daddy up and left. I know you were just bein' supportive. I'm sorry I'm such poor company." They grinned sheepishly at one another and sat at the table.

"The gumbo's just simmerin'. Would you like a beer or glass of wine? Actually, I think I even have some of ma pa's moonshine in the cellar." Patrick shook his head quickly.

"No, no thank you. Just water will be fine." Sarah Jane's smile widened further.

"Not much of a drinkin' man?" she asked as she went to the small fridge and retrieved a pitcher of lemon water.

"No," he replied simply.

<u>Upstate</u>
One Year Prior
"That was a wonderful service, Pastor Pat! I hope you and Cynthia will join us for brunch today" The Bransons were smiling hopefully at him and his instinct was to decline but Cynthia was pinching his arm ruthlessly.

"We would be honored to join you, Joe! Thank you so much for your continued support and Lana, your brownies were the biggest hit at the bake sale yesterday! I think you singlehandedly made our goal happen!" Cynthia cut in, beaming. "What can we bring?"

The couple and Cynthia continued to chat and Patrick wandered off toward the playground. The Bransons had invited them to brunch every single Sunday since Patrick had become Pastor and he had always managed to avoid their invites.

"It's awful manners, Patrick! You must think of what the members of this parish do for our church. Next time they ask us, you better accept!" Cynthia had warned him just before the service that morning. Patrick had merely nodded but he had no intention of doing what she suggested. Of course Cynthia knew that and had made it a point to be at his side afterward. He was beginning to find himself irritated with his wife over the tiniest issues. But he had found a way to cope with her annoying habits. As he watched the children playing happily on the monkey bars, he forced his mind out of the spot where it always went and circled back to the rear entrance of the church. The fire door was open and he slipped inside, unnoticed. He made his way to his office and secured the door behind him. Then he dropped tiredly into the high back leather chair and unlocked the bottom drawer to his desk. He pulled open the mickey of vodka and took a huge swig. He paused for a moment and after the burning sensation in his throat passed, he helped himself to one more before replacing the bottle and popping cough drop into his mouth. Well at least there would be mimosas at brunch.

<u>Down South</u>

Sarah Jane had not exaggerated her culinary talents; the gumbo was phenomenal. She had even set up a bowl for Jamba which the dog inhaled in three bites and begged for seconds. As Sarah Jane had anticipated, Damien did reappear before dinner was through. He ignored both of the adults and sat on the floor to play with Jamba who relished the attention.

"So do ya do fer a livin', Patrick?" Sarah Jane inevitably asked. Patrick considered lying but there was something about this woman that made him want to only speak in truths.

"I was a pastor but I'm not really doing anything at the moment," he responded, looking down at his bowl. Sarah Jane's face seemed to light up like a Christmas tree.

"Y'all must be really smart then!" she exclaimed. Patrick laughed.

"Well I wouldn't go that far!"

"Y'all gone to college, ain't ya?" Patrick nodded.

"Would y'all be willin' ta help me with schoolin' Damien? I ain't so good in English an' history an' artsy stuff. I kin hold ma own in math and science but spellin' dang if I don't go messin' everythin' up!" Patrick was taken aback by the offer.

"Well, I..."

"Oh, I kin pay ya! I'm a researcher actually. I do online consultin' for some huge firms so money ain't really a problem."

"I would be happy to help you with Damien," Patrick responded. "If Damien would be willing to have me. Damien, would you mind if I come and help with some of your lessons?"

The child looked completely startled at being addressed. He stared at Patrick with hole boring black eyes and then, after what seemed like an eternity, he shrugged, barely nodded and turned back to Jamba.

"Well I guess it's settled then! When do we start?"

The following morning, Patrick woke to contractors on the roof. The pale morning light was sparkling through the trees and despite his sore back from sleeping on the rough wood pallet in one of the two bedrooms, he felt elated for the first time in as long as he could remember. Even Jamba seemed contented as she followed him to the outhouse. He walked down toward the water, keeping a watchful eye out for alligators and splashed some cool water on his face before retreating back to the cottage. He dug a pair of jeans and a t-shirt out of the suitcase and quickly changed before leaving the construction crew and heading to meet Sarah Jane and Damien. He thought about the developmentally challenged little boy and wondered about Sarah Jane's husband. He wondered if a father would have changed the child's life substantially. He angrily pondered what kind of man would abandon a boy who needed more support than the average child and leave the mother alone to contend with the aftermath. Then he thought about Cynthia.

<u>Upstate</u>
<u>Fifteen Years Prior</u>

"Are you happy, Patrick?" she asked as they drove home from the cabin. She seemed annoyed at having spent part of their honeymoon in the swamp but she didn't say anything out loud.

"Of course I'm happy! I've married my queen, we're starting our lives together upstate where we'll have a gaggle of babies and we are going to live happily ever after! How could I be anything but ecstatic? How about you? Any regrets yet?" He grinned teasingly at her and Cynthia flashed him a brief smile.

"Of course I am!" She turned to watch the gorgeous scenery. "Patrick?"

"Yes, my love?"

"I need to tell you something."

"You can tell me anything. I am your husband." He grinned wider as he said the word. He loved the way it sounded. "Husband. I like the sound of that. I wonder if I'm going to like the sound of 'daddy' as much. Probably. I guess we'll find out."

"Patrick, I had an accident when I was young, I fell off a horse," Cynthia said quietly. "And the doctor's have told me that I can't have children."

<u>Ten Years Prior</u>

His head was pounding. He hadn't had a migraine since his late teens but the air pressure was affecting his blood pressure and he was suffering terribly.

"Cyndi? Cynthia?" he croaked from the bedroom but there was no answer. Only Jamba lay on the pillow beside him, nuzzling his neck. "Cyndi?"

She must have gone out while I was sleeping, he thought. The thought of getting out of the bed was agonizing but he had no choice. He slowly and painfully rose to his feet, trying to move as gingerly as possibly. The nausea was overwhelming but he needed to take some Aspirin before the pain got much worse or else he would end up hospitalized. Slowly, he shuffled into the bathroom and tried to remember where Cynthia kept the pain medication. He was unaccustomed to taking any form of medicine. He began rummaging through drawers when the cabinet in the bathroom produced no results. He found himself in Cynthia's beauty products when his hand closed around a circular package. When he looked down at it, he thought the pain had affected his vision but the logical, educated side of him knew what he was staring at birth control pills. His wife had been taking birth control pills.

Five Years Prior

The party was in full swing and while everyone was having a grand old time, Patrick had one of his now trademark headaches. He looked around everywhere for Cynthia but he couldn't find her. Finally, he escaped to the backyard for some fresh air and snuck around to the side of the house. What he saw made his blood run cold; Cynthia was passionately kissing a man he considered to be one of his best friends. And Patrick slowly backed away and never mentioned the scene to anyone.

Down South

When Patrick appeared at the door, Damien actually smiled at him for the first time and he felt his heart swell. He realized that the child was more likely smiling at Jamba but Patrick still took it as a positive sign. The boy allowed them into the house and led them to a sunroom in the rear of the house. Sarah Jane was waiting for them there with coffee and fresh fruit for breakfast. The room was designed to be an educational but stimulating environment. The windows overlooked the bayou and all of the day creatures were peeking out of their hiding spots for the day. A black and white board were set up as to not obstruct the stunning view. Sarah Jane had already laid out the lessons for the day and Damien took his seat in an old style school desk. They started with a basic math lesson and Patrick was pleased to see how quickly Damien finished his assignments. The child had a natural knack for math and science. *Just like his mother*, Patrick thought with appreciation. He was warmed as he saw the interaction between mother and son. While Damien was non-verbal, the managed to communicate through gestures and he genuinely seemed to hang on to her every word. When it came Patrick's time to take stage, he began with one of his sermons, one that young Austin had liked so much, David and Goliath. He noted happily that Damien was enraptured by the story and afterward they took a break for lunch.

Damien took his tuna fish sandwiches outside to share with Jamba while Sarah Jane and Patrick sat in the cozy kitchen and talked. To Patrick's surprise, he found himself opening up to her about Cynthia, things he had never shared with anyone. She in turn talked about Damien's father and they both felt a deep connection to one another through the strangers they had married. They talked about their spouses openly.

"Damien's daddy was neva any good at facin' problems," Sarah Jane said. "I guess I shoulda seen that before we got hitched. He drank like a fish and got inta all kinds of bar fights but I was all struck by them big ole black eyes and them pretty white teeth. As soon as he realized Damien wasn't like other boys, he hightailed it outta town lickity split. Neva heard a word from him in ova five years now. Ain't no big loss. Damien an' I always did okay together."

"Even after I discovered that Cynthia had been lying to me on so many levels, I still wanted to be a good husband to her. I really did love her. Or at least the woman I believed she was. Aside from that one horrible, stupid night, I was never unfaithful to her. I never even considered it."

They smiled at each other and Patrick reached across the table to put his hand over hers.

"We do the best we can given what we got," Sarah Jane told him, giving his palm a gentle squeeze.

"And remember that God won't ever throw anything at us we can't handle," Patrick replied.

The days were long and wonderful, filled with lessons for Damien and walks through the swampland. The contractors finished the cabin and there was finally a bathroom, electricity and running water within its walls. Even Jamba was thriving in her new environment, attempting to befriend the racoons and once even a gator. The nights were less and less lonely, spent playing Monopoly with Damien and Sarah Jane. When the boy would go to bed, Sarah Jane and Patrick would talk until the wee hours of the morning, listening to the fish splashing in the water and the crickets chirping. They never seemed to run out of subjects to discuss. Sarah Jane was worldly and intelligent and a wonderful conversationalist. Once in a while they would drive into town and see a film at the small outdoor theater or go for ice cream. Sarah Jane and Patrick would stroll arm in arm and sometimes, Patrick would feel a small hand slip into his for a moment or two and then Damien would run off to be with Jamba.

One morning, a courier pulled up on the dirt road outside of the cabin just as Patrick was leaving for Sarah Jane's house. His heart in his throat, Patrick opened the screen and accepted the registered letter. A bittersweet feeling overwhelmed him as he tore open the envelope. It was the final divorce decree, signed by Cynthia. He put the paper back in the casing and slowly made his way up the road. When Sarah Jane opened the door, she noticed his serious expression.

"What's wrong?"

"I got my final divorce papers today."

A smile lit up her entire face.

"Ya don't say! So did I!" She reached out to a coffee table and produced a letter of her own.

"Jus' after y'all got here, I decided to start lookin' for Damien's daddy to end this charade once and fer all. I found 'im and I had him served with papers! Don't God act in mysterious ways sometimes?" Patrick felt all of his doubts disappear. He grabbed Sarah Jane by the waist, brushed her dark hair from her blue eyes and beamed down at her lovingly.

"I love you, Sarah Jane," he whispered. Then he leaned in and gently placed a sweet kiss upon her lips.

"Pa...pa...pa...!" They both turned to look at Damien who had appeared in the doorway to the kitchen, pointing at Patrick.

"Oh! Damien is trying to say my name!" he almost yelled and quickly threw his hand over his mouth worried about startling the boy. Sarah Jane smiled dreamily at him.

"No, honey. I think he's trying to call you 'pa.' Will you be my boy's pa?"

And Patrick could not remember a time when his heart had been so full, his life so complete. *Thank you, lord, for giving me another chance at happiness.*

"Only if his mother will agree to be my wife."

NEVER ALONE

DEANN POCHE

Thunder sounded overhead, waking her up. Marlene rolled over in bed and looked out the window. The night sky was as black as she had ever seen. Heavy, deeply colored storm clouds swirled overhead. Whistling winds shook the branches of the tree near her window, making them dance.

She opened her eyes and could still see it in her mind's eye. The brown container sitting on the top shelf in the bathroom cabinet. She could hear it calling out to her as she laid in bed staring at the ceiling fan. The temptation resonated from the cavernous space under the sink, bounced against the walls of the hallway, and echoed in her mind.

Just one pill won't hurt.

She shook her head no. But one pill would lead to another

And Marlene felt weak.

She couldn't remember the last time she slept without those pills calling out to her, begging for attention. She wanted to lie in bed, ignore it and or just throw it away.

But she couldn't do that. She needed it as a safety net.

She pulled the sheets off her body and tossed them off the bed.

Her feet dragged across the carpet as she entered the dark bathroom. She turned the light on and the felt the cold of the tile floor attack her feet.

Marlene opened the medicine cabinet and saw the pills staring back at her.

"Only one a day," she remembered the doctor saying. Her words were innocuous but the tone in which she delivered it made it sound like a curse. She described the possible after effects and Marlene felt shivers going down her spine.

She grabbed the bottle and opened the cap. She wondered when her hands had become so thin.

No. Not today.

Marlene placed the bottle of pills back on the shelf.

I won't throw it away. But I'll make through today.

Marlene then went back to bed. She tried to clear her mind through prayer and positive thoughts.

It didn't work. She just laid there and closed her eyes, seeing nothing but the endless black of her loneliness.

Marlene must have read C.S.Lewis' *A Grief Observed* a dozen times since it happened. She remembered that a teacher had given it to her when her father died when she was thirteen years old. The book wasn't much help then and it didn't help now. She just read and re-read hoping that she was missing something because three other women at her church raved about it.

She remembered the day her father died. A sparrow had crashed up against their window and fell to the ground. She picked up the bird and took it to her father who was working in the shed. He gave the bird the once over and said they could try and nurse it back to health. Her father said that the bird just needed a rest and that it would be okay in the morning. They placed the bird into a shoebox and waited.

The next morning, her father would be found dead of a heart attack. The bird would be found dead in the shoebox.

Marlene remembered how her mother refused to move her father's chair from its corner space in the living room. The chair was ratty, her mother had upholstered it haphazardly with a staple gun. She would also clean it obsessively to the point where Marlene got sick to her stomach watching her mother repeatedly wash down and clean the old chair.

But now that Tom was out of her life, Marlene understood her mother's obsession.

She wished she could find something, anything of Tom that she could wash down and clean. His dirty clothes. Shoes. Anything.

Her friend Carol had called and left numerous messages. She knew she should call her back but put it off. She didn't even log into her Facebook. Ever since Tom left she felt that she didn't need anyone, anymore. People were a social obligation she didn't need or want. She was a loner at heart but with Tom, she could be herself. She could even socialize at family gatherings and church socials because she could feed off his positivity. Now, she couldn't see how she could sustain a conversation with anyone.

Marlene always liked people despite her introversion. She liked the church. But sometimes she just wanted to sit in silence and wait, listening, hoping that somewhere in the silence her father would reach out and whisper to her.

He never did.

And now she hoped that Tom would do what her father never did.

Marlene entered *Le Bouc* at exactly six o'clock in the evening.

The same restaurant where they had their first date, they would come there for special occasions.

She had forgotten what they had ordered . Lost in the fog of war, they were never a couple to order the same thing from the menu.

Just the same location.

She never really noticed the décor until now. The blue table clothes and tall water glasses spoke of an elegant dining experience. A place to be shared with someone.

A waitress came to her table. Her name tag read Tina and she wore a t-shirt that said I Heart Paris. She looked to be in her mid-twenties. Very cheerful.

Her happiness made Marlene feel even sadder.

"Hi there," Tina slid the menu on Marlene's table while filling her glass with water. "Anything else I can get you before you decide?"

"I'm waiting for someone," Marlene said. "Thanks."

"No worries."

The restaurant smelled like fresh lilac and summer despite the winter weather outside.

The minutes went by. Then an hour. Every now and then the waitress would walk by and give her a polite smile as she helped other diners. Her demeanor was deferential and polite to all. But Marlene noticed that while she was away from patrons she would smack the gum in her mouth.

Tom would never be late. If anything, he would always be early. She liked that about him. How he did a "recon" mission for every place they went. He would check out a new restaurant, new gym, any kind of new place beforehand before taking her there. Maybe it was part of his persona or his Army Ranger training. He always paid attention to detail and had an obsessive nature to plan everything in advance.

But everything would not always go as planned.

She looked across at the empty seat opposite her. How many times did they sit across from each other and waste precious time arguing about petty stuff? Well, she would argue and he would either get quiet or laugh it off. She would give anything to take it all back.

She looked over at the couple sitting two tables away from her. The man idly looked out the window at the slight drizzle coming down. The woman had her Smartphone on the table, sliding through screen menus while nibbling at a salad.

The only sounds coming from the table was their forks hitting the plates.

Marlene opened her purse and saw the tube of pills on the side. She willfully ignored the temptation and took out her hand mirror.

She looked even worse than she felt. Bone-tired. Her short brown hair looked limp and lifeless against her head. Her hazel eyes, which Tom would always describe as 'the most beautiful eyes he'd ever seen' now looked flat and bloodshot from carrying heavy bags beneath them. Her skin seemed dull, even yellow, and her cheeks looked sunken.

Her reflection in the mirror reflected how she felt on the inside.

"Sweetling," a deep voice came from behind her. The sound of his voice made the hairs on the back of her neck stand up.

Startled, she looked back and watched as Tom sat down opposite her.

"You came," Marlene said.

"Of course," Tom said.

"I can't believe it."

"I can't believe you did what you did," Tom said.

He looked younger than she remembered him. He wore no coat, just that blue denim shirt that she had purchased for him years ago. It looked fresh off the rack. He looked to have regained a lot of the muscularity from his youth. Tom had these crinkles at the corners of his crystal-blue eyes like he always did. It came from smiling a lot. His golden skin was covered in sun freckles. That was the contrast between he and her. The sun kissed his skin and brought out all of these light brown freckles over his face while Marlene's skin was pale and white like the color of icing on a cake.

A cross pendant dangled from his neck. That was new.

"I wanted to-" Marlene said.

"Wanted to what?" Tom asked. It had been only months but it felt like years since she had last seen him. He still retained that ease about him, that air that floated around him seeming lighter than the air that she breathed. He didn't notice anything or anyone outside of her.

"I didn't do it to get attention. I don't know why. A bird flew up against my window and it fell to the ground. I couldn't breathe. I just watched it, laying there. Like it did it on purpose. I guess it gave me a flashback."

"I'm sorry to hear that."

"You just left me out of the blue," Marlene said. "There was no warning. No letter. No nothing. I don't even remember what our last conversation was about."

"Does it matter?"

"Yes. Everything matters."

"How about this?" Tom turned to the window and then back at Marlene. "We talked about the weather. How much you loved the rain. Not stormy weather. But just a light drizzle. Because when we took a walk around the pond it would be just us. Us and the ducks. Then we make our way to that cherry tree garden and see the blossom's bloom. We sit by the pond and talk. Remember that time the turtle came out from the pond?" Tom smiled, tilting his head to try and get Marlene to look him in the eye.

"And we'll never get to do that again," Marlene she said with bitterness.

Tom shook his head as if fighting away dark thoughts.

Marlene stood up from the table. She began to walk away but Tom got up and grabbed her arm.

"Please," he said. "I've come a long way."

"You left me," she said. "Now I want to return the favor."

"Please," Tom said, waving his hand at her chair. "You didn't want to meet with me to even the score. Let's just talk. Like we used to. Come on, Beautiful."

It felt like decades since Tom had called her 'beautiful.' That was part of what attracted her to him. He had looked at her in a way that no man ever had or since. It was as if he wanted to absorb whatever kind of beauty he'd seen in her.

"I'm not beautiful anymore," Marlene said. "I'm old. I'm tired. Life hasn't been easy on me and I'm done fighting."

"Stop that. You're beautiful. You know you are."

"That didn't stop you from leaving me did it?"

"Do you remember our first date here?" Tom twirled his hand in the air. She liked that about him, how he talked with his hands. "Do you remember how you resisted going out with me at first? Jesus. I had to practically beg you to go out with me. I know if I can just take you out, you could see things my way. You see I had a vision. You only had sight."

"Is that right?"

"I saw us for what we could be. I saw that house with a flower garden. I saw those little girls we'd have chasing after butterflies in the backyard. I saw us sitting at a dinner table together, saying grace. I saw all of that. I just had to convince you to see the future with me."

Marlene slammed her fist on the table. "Things were not supposed to be this way! You didn't see that things would end up like this did you?"

The waitress came back over to the table.

"Is everything all right, ma'am?" she asked.

"Yes," Marlene took a deep breath. "I'm okay."

The waitress looked at Marlene's glass of water, hoping to refill it. Instead, she just gave a polite smile and walked away.

"I'm just so grateful," Tom said. "For everything."

"Not for me," Marlene took her purse off the table. She hugged it to her chest as if it were her lifeline. Then she reached inside and took out the bottle of pills. She unscrewed the cap but Tom took her wrist.

"It doesn't help," Tom said. "You know it won't."

"Well, maybe I'm weak like that."

"I wish I could tell you certain things," Tom said. "If you only knew...If you only knew how things will turn out."

"Another one of your visions, right?" Marlene said. "My vision was that you would be here. With me. Watching our kids grow. Watching the grandkids come. All of it. All of that."

"We had this conversation before," Tom said. "Remember? Things won't always be the way they are now. How are the kids coping?"

"They're okay, I guess. They are still in shock. You should see them."

Tom looked way and noticed a father walking into the restaurant with his family, holding hands with his young daughter.

"Do you miss us?"

Tom said nothing as the tears slowly welled in his eyes. She had never seen him like this. Tom was so full of life. She had to admit that she would often feel bland next to his vibrant persona but she loved that about him. He always seemed to make things around him a little brighter even though everything about him and his past should have been dark.

Tom was raised by a verbally abusive mother. She thought it was a sin to smile. She had a certain aura of someone who felt as if she were better than everyone. She was short with a hook nose and had hollowed out eyes. She berated him on a daily basis for whatever imagined transgression she could think of. He never knew his father.

Marlene remembered when she visited his mother's house for the first time. There were no pictures on the walls. They didn't have any family photos whatsoever. There were no snapshots of a time when anyone was happy.

Tom told her that he never truly felt happy until he met her. That made her feel special.

Tom never blamed his mother for her flaws. He told her of his upbringing and said that he didn't blame her for her weaknesses, even the ones she had passed down to him.

Still, Marlene thought that Tom was nothing like his mother. She remembered the first time she met her. She gave Marlene this dirty look as if she hated Marlene for taking her son away from her. Her cold stare bore into Marlene like she was slowly picking Marlene apart, piece by piece. Marlene almost backed out of the relationship because she didn't want to deal with such a woman but his mother would die of lung cancer a few months after they married.

Tom's mother's abusive words echoed in his head throughout his life. Marlene could see that in him some days. That woman had no doubt taken the purity and naivete out of Tom's eyes and replaced it with weariness. Once married, Marlene would do everything she could to give him back his hope, to give him back the light he had inside him. She often wondered why and how such a kind man could emerge from an abusive home. Or why he would be destined to be there in the first place.

"His ways are not our own," he whispered.

"I don't care about 'His ways,'" Marlene hissed. "I want you back."

"That's good," Tom said. "It is okay to be angry. You have to give yourself time to grieve and be angry and upset and sad."

"I left our bed unmade for two weeks. I didn't even think about it. I thought about painting the walls. I bought all this blue paint and now its just sitting there."

Marlene began to cry. She buried her head in her hands and sobbed her broken heart out. She thought she had let it out before. Days after Tom left her she had cried and cried until she thought she had no more tears left. Now a new set of tears had pooled up inside her.

He reached over and touched her hair, caressing her.

"Marlene," he said. "I miss everything. The kids. You. I miss you next to me. Your smile. Even your lousy tuna casserole. I miss the way you looked at me and the way I felt when I looked back at you. I feel an ache in my heart when I remember the last time we kissed. I wanted you to take a part of me for yourself-"

"I don't even remember the last time we kissed."

Tom looked back over at the family across the aisle. The father was making his daughter laugh, making funny faces.

"I remember the first time when I taught Jessica how to ride her bike," Tom said. "Remember that? She looked at me with these big, bright, trusting eyes like she wanted to fall into my arms because she knew I would always be there to catch her. But now-"

Marlene always loved listening to Tom talk. She found something comforting in his tone of voice, like everything in the world would turn out okay.

"Why did you leave me?"

"I can't explain-" His face looked red hot and he began fidgeting with the center button on his shirt. "I see things in a different light than before. I could spew out apologies like I was a fountain and make them flow like water." Tom picked up Marlene's glass and swirled the water around as he looked out the window at the rainy weather. "You ever wonder why no one talks about the beauty in winter. Or all those tiny changes that add up to a new season? Remember how we used to take those walks and look at the little things. The crystals of frost on the leaves that are changing colors. Or when it is so cold you can puff out a lung full of air and see your icy breath. But people forget to breathe in those special moments. They forget. I forgot."

"Do you know how hard it has been without you?" Marlene said. "I wake up in the middle of the night and think I feel you next to me. I walk downstairs in the morning and expect you to come through the door. You know, after your morning run like you used to. But now? Now everything is so quiet. The kids still call. People come around but not as much as they used to, you know? They go on with their lives."

"As they should-"

"But I can't," Marlene said.

She stared at Tom for a few moments then looked away.

"You were always the strong one," Tom said. "If the roles were reversed, I don't know if I could go on. But for you to take those pills."

Tom shook his head 'no.'

"I wanted to medicate myself," Marlene said. "I only see you in my dreams now. So now all I want to do is sleep."

"You used to glow when you slept," Tom said. "Did I ever tell you that? That's when I would hold you tighter. I wanted more of your beauty to rub off on me."

"I'm just weak. Damaged and broken. You needed someone who could be full of life and love to give you. Not just take. That is all I did. I just took."

"You're wrong. You have to think of the hurt you could have caused our kids. What would become of them if their own mother overdosed on some pills?"

"All I want to do is sleep," she whispered.

"You can't sleep," Tom said. "There's still life to be led. You have our children. They'll have grandchildren. You'll need them. They'll need you."

"I am the loneliest person on earth," Marlene said. "I go to church and feel as if I'm a dead woman walking. I mean people talk to me and I don't hear them. They all want to help. I can't hear them. I just don't know what to do."

"I want you to think about all of the times we had together," Tom said. "Jesus, we've been together for how long now? I remember when I first saw you. My friend Frank and I were on leave and he was a Christian. Told me I should go to his church but I refused. Then he told me there would be lots of pretty girls there. So I went-"

"You told me this story before-"

"But it never gets old," Tom laughed. "Because when I saw you, my heart sank. I could see you were among the popular set. I never was. There were all these All-American type people around you. I mean, they were popular, cool and sleek, like a brand new car with a brand name that everyone knew. I was a poor soldier boy."

"But you were a handsome soldier boy."

"And remember when we went to the Monterey Aquarium. Went on a work day. Had the whole place to ourselves."

"I remember."

"Do you remember this?" Tom reached over and handed Marlene a small turtle figurine made of jade.

"Oh my God," she said. "Where did you find this?"

"At the time, I had to give you something," he said. "I always felt nervous around you. You were so much more than I could ever hope to be. I didn't know if you were looking at me the same way I looked at you. So I wanted to give you something. I wanted to give you a tiny piece of myself just in case you didn't like me. I was silly, right? I mean, I thought you would keep it. Maybe not forever but at least a part of me would be with you."

Marlene twisted the wedding ring on her finger. She looked at Tom's fingers. Thick and stubby, the gold ring shining in the restaurant light.

Then she studied the figurine.

"I called it the 'promise turtle,'" Tom said, chuckling. "If a turtle swims over to you, he's giving you the blessing. I told you that we had to kiss and that our love will last forever. Remember? Then we stood in front of the aquarium and that turtle swam up and we kissed for the first time. At that moment, I knew you were the one."

"I knew it before you did."

"Okay," Tom said. "Now do you remember our wedding night?"

"Of course."

"Those are the kind of things you have to think about. Think about how it felt. Think. How did it feel?"

"It was a long time ago."

"Think," Tom whispered. "Remember."

"I felt loved," Marlene said. "I felt whole, wanted and loved. I knew there would be nothing that could tear us apart. I remember how we spent hours there, looking at one another. Smiling, cuddling, talking, sharing secrets. I remember I looked out the window when you fell asleep and the night came upon us in this gorgeous shade of dark blue."

Tom placed his hand over the turtle in her hand, squeezing. "I don't want you to be hurting. I know it is quiet. It is dark-"

"You don't know anything," Marlene pulled away and threw the figurine against the wall. She looked around, embarrassed,but saw that the restaurant was now empty. "Don't you realize those are just fading memories. "

Tom leaned back in his chair and looked at Marlene. "Not for me."

"I don't even remember the last thing I said to you. Or even the last time we kissed."

Marlene looked across at her husband. She tried hard to embed the curves of his face to her memory. Maybe he was a ghost, a figment of her imagination, invisible to anyone else.

All she knew was that her eyes burned from not wanting to blink.

"Sometimes things don't work out the way we want," Tom said. "Right now, you have the sight but not the vision. Just know that I'll always love you. What we say here on earth will not be our last words."

Marlene paused. She put her head in her hands and rubbed her eyes with her palm. Then her Smartphone buzzed. She reached into her purse.

"So sorry for your loss," a text message wrote.

"He was such a good man," another said. "Call me if you need anything."

Looking up, Marlene could only stare at the empty chair in front of her.

"Ma'am," the waitress said. "You're welcome to wait for your guest as long as you want but are you sure I can't get you anything in the meantime?"

"No," Marlene said. "I don't think he's coming. I'm sorry. I should be leaving."

"Take your time," the waitress, noticing something on the floor. "Was this yours?"

She picked up the turtle figurine and held it up.

"Yes," Marlene said. "Yes, it is. Sorry, I must have dropped it."

"Turtles were like miracles to see where I grew up," the waitress said, handing the turtle to Marlene. "I saw a turtle in a pond once. My father said that it meant that we were special because miracles are special. And not everyone is lucky enough to see one."

Marlene thanked the waitress and she walked off. Looking down, she twirled the figurine around through her fingers. Her heart was racing and the turtle felt as if it were burning a hole in her palm. Her fingers couldn't stop twitching.

Tom's words echoed in her head.

"You are special," Tom said. "We've come so far together and I'm so proud of you. Times will be hard. You'll be lonely. You'll reach out for me but you won't be able to touch me. There will be long hours of silence and some memories of our time together will fade. But I'm not a ghost. I'll always be with you. You will make it without me."

"You are strong."

Marlene went into their bedroom and shut the door quietly.

Looking out the window, she could see the sky melting into dark, rising bursts of gray, black and blue. Thunder sounded every few steps she took while the lightning made her feel like a frightened little girl.

She entered the bathroom and opened the medicine cabinet.

Then she poured all of the sleeping pills in the toilet and flushed.

The crackling of the storm began to die down.

She flicked off the lights in the room, took off her shoes and flipped them to the floor. She laid down on the large bed and looked up at the ceiling fan. She watched as the blades circled round and round until her eyes grew heavy.

She gripped the turtle figurine in her palm.

Marlene dreamed about Tom. They walked in silence on the bird trail. There was a pond inhabited by quacking ducks and trees with squirrels. The ground felt moist from rain. Marlene slipped in the mud but Tom grabbed her arm and straightened her up. They both laughed and continued to walk.

The sun hung low, big and bright, it separated the clouds. The colors were like a kaleidoscope painted across the sky.

Tom looked up and watched the sun set.

He told Marlene that he needed to go back home.

They walked together in silence back down the trail. It was a comfortable silence, the way old trees stood tall next to one another, their roots twining into one, over time, and never having to speak.

Tom glanced over at Marlene ever so often, as if watching over her. She would turn back at him, and their eyes locked.

Tom's fingers slipped into her hair before gave her one last kiss.

He kissed Marlene like the ocean kisses the sands on the shore of a beach when the tide comes in.

He called her name between breaths. Their lips touched one last time.

Then he went home, into the sun.

THE WEDDING DRESS

GIGI GROSS

Chapter 1

Gabriela stared at her bank account, willing it to change. There was no way she was down to a hundred and twenty dollars. She wasn't getting paid for another three days! Even when she did get paid, a majority of it would get eaten up by her rent and groceries for that week. "Oh no," Gabriela said, laying her head on her arms. She didn't want to think about it, or look at it, or have anything to do with it. Unfortunately, when the problems are in your own life, you cannot exactly run away from them.

Gabriela wanted to call Bryan and get his support. She knew he would have all the verbal support she could want, but he wouldn't be able to loan her any money. His financial situation was just as bad as hers and he made even less money than she did. Once again, Gabby re-evaluated the idea of moving in with Bryan already. It would save them a few hundred bucks a month, and it wasn't so bad. After all, everyone was doing it.

"Maybe then, I would actually have money for a wedding dress," Gabby muttered to herself.

"Having a conversation with yourself again?" Reese asked her.

Gabby quickly minimized her bank account window. "Yes," she replied, trying to put aside her doubts to talk to her sister.

"You're starting to worry me. Turn that frown upside down!" Reese said, coming over and hugging Gabby.

Gabby couldn't help shaking her head and allowing a small smile to form on her lips. "Thanks, Reese." Reese started playing with Gabby's hair, brushing her fingers through its strands. Gabby closed her eyes and sunk into the sensation. It felt so calming to have her sister play with her hair as she had done since she was a little girl.

"Your graduation is in two weeks, isn't it?" Gabby asked, making slow conversation. Reese's hands felt so good.

"Yup! I can't believe I'm actually going to be done with high school. Then, I'm going to college, and that scholarship is seriously a blessing, don't you think?"

Gabby did her best at a nod. "Yes, I don't know how we would do it without that scholarship."

"Do you think Mom and Dad will come to my graduation?" Reese asked in a quiet voice. Gabby was glad she didn't have to look her sister full in the face as she answered.

"I don't know, Reese. Dad might not come because he thinks Mom will be there. Besides, he hasn't really been here for a while. I don't know. Mom might come."

"Do you think she'll bring her terrible boyfriend?"

"I don't know, Reese, but I want you to focus on your success, not on other people. You and only you have been the one responsible for getting yourself through high school. You have studied hard, and this is your time for a reward. I was thinking just you and me could go get ice cream at Scream Cream, maybe not that night but maybe the next if you are too busy partying."

Reese knew that Gabby's money situation was tight, but she just didn't know how tight. Gabby didn't dare let Reese in on the secret. They just needed to get through the summer then Reese would be in college, and Gabby would somehow pull together enough money for just a small wedding.

"When are you going to go dress shopping?" Reese asked after a few moments of silence.

"I don't know, Reese. I will be going soon. Don't worry. You will be invited."

"Yay! You know I am so excited for you! I'll still be able to come home for Thanksgiving or fall break to wherever you guys are, right?"

"Of course, Reese!" Gabby said, finally turning and looking her sister in the eye. "Come here." Even though Reese was eighteen, Gabby was still her big sister at twenty-five. "You will always be my baby," Gabby said, trying to make Reese sit on her lap.

"No!" Reese wailed. "I shall not! I am too old to be sitting on anyone's lap."

"Mmhmm," Gabby smiled mischievously. "I'll just tell that to your striking college boyfriend when you get him."

"Eww!" Reese said. "I'm not going to sit on anyone's lap."

Gabby laughed. "Sure, you say that now. Shall I videotape you saying it and show to you in five years? Come on, help me finish making that garlic bread."

Two days later, Gabby decided to pay a visit to Bryan. They wanted to have their wedding in the middle of August. At this point, they hadn't done anything more than decide it would be held on Bryan's family farm. That decision was based on the fact that it would be a free venue, including free flowers.

"Hey, Baby," Bryan said when Gabby dropped by at dinnertime. "I made something healthy for once. You should be proud of me."

Gabby laughed. "Of course, I'm proud of you. Reese and I rebelliously did not make a salad with our meal last night, so you are doing better than me."

"Come here," Bryan said, pulling her close. He gave her a sweet kiss. When he pulled back, Gabby smiled. This was why she was with him. He always made her feel at home. "Go ahead and sit down. I'll get you a drink in a minute," Bryan commanded.

Gabby took a seat and watched Bryan careen around the kitchen, pouring drinks, draining whole wheat pasta, and preparing their plates. When they finally sat down, Gabby took his hand and listened to Bryan pray. "Thank you, God, for this meal you have given us the resources to have. Please keep giving us all that we need. Amen."

The two began eating, and Gabby finally got up the nerve to bring up the old wedding topic. "Do you think we will even be ready to get married in August? That's only two and a half months away. I'm just worried that we won't have everything ready."

Bryan sighed, but Gabby knew that his frustration was not aimed at her. "I know it's stressful. But, we've almost gotten the rings paid for." Gabby realized at that moment that she forgotten to bring her ring payment that evening.

"Sorry!" Gabby interrupted. "I forgot my payment tonight. I'm getting paid tomorrow, though. I can just give you the money then, right?"

Bryan nodded. "That's fine. I know you're tight too. But, look, we'll have a beautiful meadow, rings, our pastor will come, and gorgeous wildflowers. Maybe we can ask guests to bring a dish. I know it's not conventional," Bryan said in response to Gabby's strange look. "But, maybe they will understand. Feeding so many people can be a few thousand dollars."

"I know," Gabby nodded. "And you paint a beautiful picture. I like the way it sounds. The problem is that. . .I really want to wear a special dress. I've always dreamed of a gorgeous white wedding dress, and I just don't know if I will be able to afford one. I don't want our wedding to just pass by like it's not anything special. I want to look beautiful for you." Gabby's voice cracked with emotion, and she looked down to avoid crying.

Bryan reached over and pat her hand. "I know that it is important to you. It's important to me that you have the wedding just how you want it. But I want you to know that whatever you choose to wear, I will love it." That was when Gabby realized that her yearning to wear such a beautiful gown might not be because she wanted Bryan to think she was beautiful. Maybe she just wanted to feel beautiful for once, not for anyone else but for herself.

Chapter 2

On Saturday, Gabby left Reese sleeping at home in bed to peruse the local flea market. She needed to get Reese a graduation present, but she also didn't have a lot of money to spend on something like that. She had no idea what she wanted to get her sister, but she knew that she liked to read. Perhaps, Gabby could find a few books at a reasonable price.

Gabby was looking at a table of books, holding a couple in her hands. The three books were only twelve dollars altogether, and Gabby thought they would be a great present for Reese right before her last free summer. Gabby looked up, and her eyes fell on a shining white dress hanging on a mannequin the next stall over. Gabby left the three books on the table and walked toward the dress as if in a trance.

Her hand reached up to stroke the fabric. Just as her fingers were going to touch the fabric, Gabby wondered if she should. She looked around to see if anyone was watching her. She saw a small, elderly woman with her eyes trained on her.

"Oh, sorry," Gabby said, stumbling into an apology. "I'm sorry. I didn't know if it was alright to touch, but it's so.. .pretty."

"Go ahead," the woman said in a raspy but friendly voice. "You may touch it." Her smile encouraged Gabby just the bit she needed to have the courage. She turned back to the dress and stroked it. It was soft, almost like silk. The beadwork was amazing, with little detail stitched along the folds of the fabric. The bosom was covered with exquisite beadwork, and the waist came in before flowing out in a long skirt. The train was not overwhelming but still had a presence. It was as though someone had created a wedding gown out of Gabby's imagination.

Gabby's breath caught in her throat. She didn't want to turn away from the beauty. She stealthily scanned the dress for a price tag. Of course, there was not one. That must mean that the dress was handmade and would cost even more.

"Th-thank you," Gabby said, turning away from the dress and nodding to the woman. She took a backward step away from the dress and the woman.

"Are you getting married?" the woman asked, leaning forward encouragingly.

"Yes," Gabby nodded. "But, we don't have a date yet. It will still be a few months." Finally, she shrugged her shoulders and figured she might as well ask how much the dress cost. If she didn't, she would constantly wonder. At least with a number, she could walk away from it without feeling guilty. "How much is the dress?" Gabby nodded toward the wedding dress she had been studying.

The old woman smiled and leaned back. "Oh, that dress doesn't have a price. I'm sure you noticed. It is a beautiful and priceless piece. But," the woman continued speaking before Gabby could turn away. "I will let you wear the gown for free if you promise me one thing."

"What?" Gabby whispered, unable to wait to hear her words.

"You must live out your marriage according to God's will."

"I-uh-oh," Gabby seemed unwilling to respond. "I can wear it. . .for free?"

The woman nodded. "There's a veil that goes with the dress as well, but I must have you promise that your marriage will be uplifting to God. Can you do that?"

"I promise with my whole heart," Gabby said. She couldn't control the smile that spread across her face.

The woman nodded. "Very well. God, our good Lord, will hold you to your word. Now, just give me a moment to gather the dress and package it safely. Do you have a few minutes?"

"Yes, of course!" Gabby could hardly believe her good fortune. "Do you need any help? I could help you."

"That blue bag up there on the shelf, yes, that one. That's the veil. Go ahead and get that down, will you?" Gabby strained up to reach the high shelf, took down the bag, and could not help peering into the bag to examine the veil.

"What do you think?" the woman asked, nodding at the veil.

"It's amazing," Gabby said. The woman carefully took out the veil and used the comb part to place the veil on Gabby's head. She handed Gabby a small hand-mirror, and Gabby nearly cried. She looked like a real bride, not a bride who didn't have any money. Spontaneously, Gabby reached down and hugged the old woman. "Thank you," she sobbed out. The woman patted Gabby's back.

Finally, Gabby carefully folded the veil and put it back in the bag. She then helped the woman take the dress off the mannequin and store it in a garment bag.

"I have one more thing for you," the woman said as Gabby prepared to leave. The woman pulled out a thick book. "I want you to take a look at this. This dress, you see, has a long history. It has made many brides happy on their wedding day, and they all needed it in one way or another. I encourage you to find out about their stories and write your own as well."

Gabby took the thick, leather bound book in the crook of her arm and tried to give the woman one last hug while balancing her packages. "How will I find you again?" Gabby asked.

"I'm always right here," the woman assured her. "Come back after your wedding, and I'll be waiting."

Gabby smiled, thanked the woman one more time, then hurried out of the flea market, forgetting all about Reese's graduation present. The smile could not be wiped off her face. She carefully laid the dress across her backseat and could not help but sing along with every song on the radio. The only thing left to do was try it on. When she reached home, she carried the dress inside and explained the whole story to Reese who at first felt deceived that her sister had gone wedding dress shopping without her.

"I'm going to try it on," Gabby said. "Wait until I'm in it, okay? Don't come in!" Gabby shut the door with her sister outside and changed as carefully as she could into the wedding dress. Gabby could tell the dress had had sleeves at some point. But, it was now a sleeveless dress. The hem was a little long, but Gabby knew she could fix that. Around her waist, the dress fit perfectly. Gabby tucked the veil into place then opened the door with a smile.

"Sis!" Reese said. The smile filling her face was all that Gabby needed to see. "It's perfect isn't it?"

"Yes, it is!" Reese gave Gabby a hug. "I can't believe you are actually getting married!"

"It seems real now."

"It is real," Reese said. "I know Bryan would love you in this dress. I wish he could see it now."

"I know!" Gabby laughed. "But it has to be our secret. "No words to him about it. None, do you hear me?"

Later that night, Bryan came over. He got along well with Reese, and Gabby loved that about him. After all, she might not be Reese's official guardian, but she was Reese's home ever since their parents had started their incessant bickering.

The three were playing a game of Phase 10, and Reese kept smiling randomly at Gabby. "Is something wrong with you?" Bryan asked her. "Or do you two have a cheat going on?"

Both Gabby and Reese laughed. "Nope, we're not cheating," they said in unison.

"Okay, because that denial was totally believable. Come on, I know something is up." Gabby looked at Reese. They both shrugged, but Gabby could not longer keep the news in.

"I got my wedding dress today," Gabby said.

"What?! That's amazing, Gabby. Where is it? Can I see it? Was it expensive?"

"To all of those questions, the answer is no. Besides, the groom is never supposed to see the dress before the wedding day."

"I've got an idea," Bryan said, leaning forward. "Want to get married tomorrow?"

"Sorry," Gabby shook her head. "Pastor is occupied tomorrow. Besides, I'm not ready yet."

"Aw," Bryan visibly drooped. "I guess we should probably wait until we have rings, huh?"

"That would be important!" Gabby said. She gave Bryan a playful kiss and was glad that she did not feel as desperate for a dress as she had that morning.

Chapter 3

Gabby carefully opened the book the woman had given her the day before. In the excitement of trying on the dress and spending time with Bryan, she hadn't thought about it again until she and her sister were leaving church. She hadn't told her sister about the book or how exactly she had gotten the dress, but she had told her enough to be satisfied.

The book appeared to be some sort of journal. On the pages were handwritten notes, some in cursive, some printed, and clearly not all done by the same person. Beside each handwritten note was a picture of a woman wearing the wedding dress. Gabby ran her hands over the first picture. The dress had had sleeves, just as Gabby suspected. The picture looked old, and it was worn around the edges. But it had stayed faithfully in the book. Beside it was a note.

"Teresa Daniels, age twenty-four. Married to Bertram Frantz, age twenty-four, on May 7, 1978. My parents had both died when I was five. I had been living with a family friend since then. The boy I grew up living next to asked me to marry him, but I didn't have any money for a wedding, let alone a beautiful dress. I met this wonderful young woman who loaned me a dress that she had just finished making. She told me to tell my story and live my marriage in a way that would make God pleased with me. I am determined to do just that. My adoptive parents may not have enough money to pay for a wedding, but this wedding dress shows just how much God is looking out for us."

Underneath the note was Teresa Frantz's contact information. In different handwriting was a little note that said she had died in a car accident in 2004. Gabby suddenly felt as though she was holding something very sacred. The dress was only used perhaps once a year, if that, and Gabby hungrily read through each story. Each woman had something to say about how she did not have enough money or something had befallen her. Gabby wondered why their contact information was there. Did they really want someone to talk to them? And what did they want to talk about?

Gabby pictured herself eight years from now with a few small children. She would always remember how she had gotten her wedding dress. What would she say to someone else who was going to use it? Gabby could only smile.

She selected two of the most recent weddings and decided to write to their email addresses. Her message was simple.

"Hi, my name is Gabriela. I'm going to use the wedding dress. I found your information in the book, and I was wondering if you'd like to meet and have a coffee."

Gabriela went to bed at close to two in the morning. "I am so not going to be awake for work in the morning," Gabby said. She had received her payment in her account over the weekend, and Gabby spent a little time that Monday morning paying her bills. It was just as nasty as ever. Even though she had a wedding dress now, she still would not be able to save any money after paying everything necessary. She sighed and shook her head. "It's okay," she told herself.

The workday passed well enough, but Reese was celebrating when she got home because she only had two more exams before she was officially done with school. Gabby spent some of the evening quizzing Reese before she gave herself the luxury of checking her email. She had received a reply.

"It's nice to hear from you, Gabriela. I would love to meet for coffee. How does Wednesday at lunch hour sound? Would it be possible for me to meet you at the Starbucks in Clayton?

Annabel"

Gabriela rejoiced over the email. She couldn't wait to meet this woman and unravel a bit more of the dress mystery.

When it finally came time for her Wednesday lunch hour, Gabby drove as quickly as she could to the Starbucks. She ordered and looked around for Annabel. She finally found her, and the two shook hands in a formal manner.

"I'm so glad you reached out and contacted me," Annabel said. "I wondered if anyone ever would."

Gabby smiled excitedly. "I can't believe the dress was first loaned out in 1978. It still looks so new."

"Well," Annabel surmised. "The sleeves were taken off, and I think some extra beadwork was added."

"Still," Gabby smiled. "It's like I'm wearing a little bit of history."

Annabel laughed. "Yeah, it's magical the way that woman wants to help us. It's like she can just sense the desperation in someone."

"So, what's your story?" Gabby asked, wanting to fill in the blanks Annabel's note had left.

Annabel nodded. "I was eighteen when I got the wedding dress. I know, I was young. I didn't want to get married yet, but my boyfriend had gotten me pregnant. I had just found out a few days before. I had talked to my boyfriend, and he and I decided we would just have a quiet wedding, a justice of the peace deal. I didn't want to do that, but I knew we needed to do something quickly. I didn't want to be one of those boldly pregnant brides. But I was so frustrated with the whole situation, that I had just decided I would wear an old dress. It didn't matter.

"When I saw that wedding dress, though, I couldn't help but be drawn to it. When the woman told me it was free for my use as long as I lived a godly marriage, I couldn't believe my good fortune. We had a justice of the peace wedding, but I was wearing a gorgeously beautiful wedding gown. I will never forget that woman's generosity." Annabel shook her head.

"So, it made your day magical?" Gabriela asked in excitement.

Annabel laughed aloud. "Yes, it sure did. My wedding may not have been what I had imagined it to be when I was fifteen or sixteen, but it was much better than it would have been under the circumstances. Now, I have Gracen, and she's getting close to her second birthday."

"Wow! That's so amazing."

"What's your story?" Annabel leaned forward and listened as Gabriela told her about her all the financial troubles she had had. Gabriela and Annabel continued chatting until the last possible minute.

"I really need to get back to my job," Gabby said, "Or I could lose it. That is definitely not what I need right now. Look, I really enjoyed talking to you. Maybe we could get together again, and I could meet Gracen?"

"I'd like that," Annabel said. "I'll talk to you later."

Chapter 4

Gabriela finally got a reply from the other woman she had contacted about meeting: Brianne. Brianne's story had seemed really tragic, and Gabriela couldn't wait to hear about it from the woman's lips.

After the introductions, Gabriela leaned forward for Brianne's story. "I'm really glad you wanted to talk," Brianne said. "I feel like this dress has created a secret group."

"Have you ever talked to Annabel?" Gabriela asked.

"Annabel. . .Annabel. I don't think so. Was she married after me?"

"I don't remember," Gabriela said. "But I have her number. Maybe we could all three get together or even more brides."

Brianne smiled. "I like the idea. I am definitely willing to contribute. Okay, so here's what happened to me. My problem was not so much a financial one as I read in so many stories. Instead, my problem was a big fire. About five days before the date our wedding was set, some sort of electrical malfunction sparked in our house. My family lost everything. Insurance took care of the problem financially, but the dress I had so carefully picked out months before along with my shoes and veil had been consumed by the fire. Trying to get a dress five days before a wedding is pretty much impossible.

"But, this beautiful old lady performed a miracle. She let me borrow the dress. It was much better than the dress I had originally picked. Better than that, it was ready for the wedding two days early." Brianne shook her head. "I had thought I might need to call off the wedding. I was freaking out. I couldn't even go to work I was so stressed out. I had a few burn marks from escaping the house, but the dress covered them nicely. They can't even be seen in the photos."

"Wow!" Gabby said, soaking in her new friend's story. "Wow." She was silent for a few minutes as Brianne's story sunk in. "Did you know that there have been thirty-three weddings in that dress? I'll be number thirty-four."

"When is your wedding?" Brianne asked.

"It'll be mid-August, right after my sister moves into her college dorm. She's been living with me."

"Would you mind if I rudely invited myself to your wedding?" Brianne smiled.

Gabby laughed. "Of course not. You are welcome. It's going to be a small wedding, and we ask that each guest bring a dish of food, a sort of potluck. We really don't have the money for much more, but I would be honored for you to come."

After meeting the two brides, Gabby wanted to meet more. She kept setting up even more appointments with brides. She had one last meeting planned before her wedding. This meeting took a few weeks to set up. By the time Gabby met her, it was the first day of August.

"What's your story?" Gabby asked impatiently. The question had become one of which she could not wait to ask each new woman. Hallie had been married almost ten years ago.

"My story's probably a bit different from some others," Hallie shook her head. Gabby had agreed to come to her house because Hallie had three young children. Hallie wanted them to be able to play and stay out of their hair while the two women talked. "I was poor. I couldn't buy a wedding dress. That much is as normal as for any of us women."

Gabby nodded, anticipating more.

"My story becomes interesting after I married Mark. Did the lady have you make a promise?"

Gabby nodded. "Yes, I promised that I would live my marriage according to God's will."

Hallie accepted Gabby's words. "Yes, I promised the same thing. At the time, I promised it because it seemed such an easy exchange for the dress. But it wasn't as easy as I thought it would be. The first year of marriage was so difficult. I looked back on the innocence I sported on my wedding day, and I would shake my head. How had I thought I loved Mark?" Hallie was quiet as she remembered. "I was sure that we were going to get a divorce. You see, his family lives on the other side of the country. I know he was really close to them, but he agreed that living here would be the best solution for us.

"But, it was like he had forgotten that. We argued almost every night. I started to hate him. He made me cry so much." Hallie shook her head, and Gabby should see the tears brimming in her eyes. "I started fantasizing about running away and going a place where he wouldn't find me. Then, I remembered my promise. I tried to weasel my way out of it, saying that the fighting was Mark's fault. I blamed him, but I knew I needed to take credit for my part. So, I started serving Mark instead of myself.

"Even when I was tired, I would make dinner. I would clean up without complaint. He noticed after a month, and I felt him become more tender toward me. We were finally able to talk through what had been happening. That was the best day of my life, the day that we finally talked it all through without screaming. I finally slept next to him and felt connected to him again.

"Gabby, that promise is going to be hard to keep. You will probably get angry with your fiance sometimes, but don't walk away. The weak walk away; it's the strong that keep fighting."

Gabby hugged Hallie as a few tears spilled over. "Thank you, Hallie. I needed to hear those words. They were just what I needed." Before Gabby left Hallie's house, she invited her to her wedding. "I know it is only two weeks, but if you think you can come, I would really like it. Don't be shy about bringing your husband and children."

Chapter 5

On the day of her wedding, Gabby carefully donned the dress. It was to be a simple ceremony. Only her sister would stand beside her. Bryan was having his best friend stand beside him. At that moment nothing felt simple about Gabby as she waited for Reese to calmly do up the back.

"I can't believe it's really the day," Gabby said.

Reese smiled. "Yeah, I'm pretty sure I'm having the most exciting first weekend home from college out of all of my friends." Of course, her statement made Gabby start asking about all of Reese's new friends. She had to make sure that her baby sister was doing well and having fun in college.

"Is it done?" Gabby asked.

Reese nodded. "It's done. You're all ready."

"Well, not completely," Gabby said. "I look fine, but I feel a bit nervous about walking down that aisle."

"Why?" Reese asked. "Are you unsure about Bryan?"

"No," Gabby shook her head. "I know he is perfect for me, well, as perfect a fit as someone can be with my rather strange personality."

Reese laughed. "Then, what is making you nervous?"

"I guess it just hit me that this is a lifelong commitment. I love Bryan, and I just don't want anything to go wrong. What if we start living together, and he does annoying things that get on my nerves?"

"Like what?"

"Like leave his socks on the bed."

"Then tell him to take his socks off," Reese shrugged. "It's not that hard. Look, if you love him and you know that for sure, then you just have to go through the bad stuff and remember that. Then you'll get to the good times, and it'll be all worth it."

"Alright, my sister the wise," Gabby smiled. "What time is it?"

Reese looked at her phone. "We still have thirty minutes."

"What a long thirty minutes that'll be!" Gabby sighed, carefully sitting in her dress.

Reese laughed aloud. "I thought you just said you were nervous to do it, and now you can't wait to go down the aisle."

Gabriela laughed with her sister. "When you get to this point, I will be right by your side and remind you of everything you just said. Meanwhile, you'll just be like. No, I'm nervous! Let me be nervous by myself!"

Gabriela's friend Erica burst into the bedroom just then. "Hey! Wow, Gabby! You look so amazing!" Erica was the unofficial photographer. She had a professional camera and had done some photo shoots. A free photographer was her wedding gift to her friend. "Look, we don't have a lot of time, but I wanted to get a few pictures of just you in all your bridal beauty, then maybe a few with Reese. Hey, Reese! How are you?" Erica said in one breath.

Gabby laughed. "Oh, Erica, I knew there was a good reason we were friends." Erica took all the photos she wanted with Gabby sitting, standing, lounging, smiling, and serious.

"Alright, Reese, get in there with your sister." After a few more shots, Erica hovered over to the door. "Alright, I believe we have five minutes before your little flower girl will start her march. Let's get you safely down these stairs."

Gabby carefully maneuvered the stairs with the help of her sister and friend. The stairs were not very wide and definitely not prepared to have brides tramping up and down them. She finally stood by the back doors.

"Ready?" Reese asked.

Because Gabby had decided against having their estranged father walking her down the aisle, Reese would be walking right beside her.

"I think so," Gabby answered. "But ask me again in a minute, and I might have a different answer."

"You've got this, Sis."

"Thanks."

Erica reappeared as the music started to assist the flower girl on her way. Next went the ringbearer. After that came Gabby and Reese. It was a simple, small wedding, just as Gabby had dreamed it. Best of all was Bryan's face when she came through the doors of the back of the farmhouse.

His smile was genuine and delighted, and Gabby looked only at him as Reese guided her steps down the aisle. When she reached the altar, she placed her hands in Bryan's, smiling into his eyes and wondering how she had ever doubted her decision to marry him.

"I love you," she whispered as the pastor was talking to them. He mouthed the words back and gave her hands a squeeze. Suddenly, the ceremony, including a candle lighting, a song sung by a friend, and a short talk from the pastor seemed all too long to Gabby. After what seemed an eternity, the words she had wanted to hear for so long pierced her thoughts.

"You may now kiss the bride."

Gabby kissed Bryan, leaning into his lips. When they pulled back, Gabby felt the magic of the moment lingering. "You're my husband," she whispered, incredulous.

"And you, my dear, are my wife." Bryan let go of one of her hands, facing the audience. The pastor announced them, and Bryan paused before they started down the aisle. "This is my wife!" he shouted, his pleasure clear as he lifted up their joined hands in victory. Gabby started laughing. Suddenly, a huge cheer rose up from the back of the rows of seats. Gabby looked over and counted five of the former brides that she had met.

"Yes, Gabriela!" They screamed together. While Gabby had not pictured her wedding as loud as a ballgame, she couldn't help laughing aloud.

Bryan carefully led her down the steps, and they entered the old farmhouse. As soon as they were inside, Bryan turned to her and kissed her passionately. "You are the most beautiful bride I have ever seen," he whispered. "And tonight, I will make you mine." Gabby trembled with anticipation, leaning in for another kiss.

A week later, Gabby carefully zipped the wedding dress into the garment bag for the last time. She took out the book and carefully glued in a photo of herself wearing the dress. She smiled at the photo then took up a pen and began writing in her best cursive beside the photo.

"Gabriela Winfox, age twenty-five. Married to Bryan Davis on August 21, 2016. This dress changed my life. Not only did it give me a chance to have the kind of wedding I would never have had on my budget, but it showed me the friendliness and generosity this kind of world doesn't see very often. It made me promise to be a more generous person and to look for opportunities to help others. I didn't have any money for a nice wedding, and my fiance and I feared we would not be able to throw a wedding. Determined to get married, because we knew it was right, I thought I would never have a wedding dress. I was wrong. Please, contact me. I would love to talk to you, and I know that the brides I met would love to talk to you as well. We are in this together."

Gabriela signed her name under her words and closed the book with a solemn thud. "Thank you, God," she said as she loaded the dress, veil, and book into the back of her car. She was on her way to the flea market.

HEART FELT

CHAPTER ONE

"Of course! Of course! I'd love to help out," Harley Harris smiled broadly but then stopped herself from looking too cheerful. She couldn't help it, whenever she got happy she looked more like an excitable ten year old girl rather than a twenty-three year old woman. "That sounds like a lot of fun."

"If you can be here, oh, tomorrow at nine? It just takes some time to set up."

Harley nodded her head. "Of course!" she said again. I can hold my end of any conversation she though sarcastically.

"Really appreciate you coming through like this," Pastor Owen said. "Theresa has been sick and she's usually in charge of stuff of the bake sale. Thanks so much."

"Of course."

Pastor Gabriel Owen was a great speaker who could be a little cold in dealing with people one on one. But once Harley got to know him she appraised him as being a great guy, just a little shy. He looked like real-life version of Yosemite Sam with his handle-bar mustache and bright red beard.

Harley thought about giving up a Saturday. She was not the party girl some of her friends were. But she needed to get out more and would take whatever kind of social engagement she could.

"And you guys will have tons of stuff to sell this year. Not just cupcakes and cookies. Steve will be on hand to help out."

"Steve?" Harley's heart began beating fast. She had no idea that Steve Forsythe would be involved.

"Yeah," Owen said.

Harley thought she caught a smirk in the pastor's face.

Steve had dated her best friend Shannon for a year before they broke up last summer. They had been the "model couple" around the church. They both looked like they could be on the poster for a

Christian dating service or a church promotional flyer. They were the beautiful people.

Until she dumped him for a high-powered attorney.

She would see Steve in church and could tell from his body language how hurt he was. She saw a terrible loneliness in his face. A decent man caught in a confusion of being involved with someone who didn't desire intimacy. He looked utterly and desperately alone. And determined to stay that way so he would never be hurt again.

She would never hurt him like that. But then again, Steve hadn't so much had looked in her direction since Shannon dumped him. He had gone way out on a barren limb and given his heart to a woman who crushed it.

Why do people treat others so bad when it came to relationships she thought. And how stupid was Shannon for dumping Steve? She was her best friend, sure, but she sure didn't appreciate a good thing when she had one. That's what really bothered Harley. How callous Shannon was in dismissing Steve and not even so much as blinking an eye. She hurt the man and now he wouldn't even look at other women.

Because Harley wanted him to look at her. And see that she was nothing like Shannon. But wouldn't even matter? She couldn't compare to Shannon when it came to looks.

Harley and Steve had been friends. She would hang out with Shannon and Steve as a threesome sometimes. He would do and say things that would make her laugh. Shannon would just stare and sometimes pout when she and Steve would "bogart the conversation" as she put it. The truth was, Harley had begun to fall for Steve and really couldn't do anything about it because of her friendship with Shannon. But now that she was out of he picture, he really didn't want anything to do with her. Did he blame her for their break-up? Did he think that she was a lot like Shannon? Materialistic and spoiled.

Harley and Shannon were best friends since the second grade. But they had grown apart after reaching their early twenties as their lives began to diverge. Shannon become more and more distant. Harley saw that Shannon viewed people in terms of their utility. If you weren't a person that she could use, than she really had no use for you.

"He'll get over it," Shannon said to Harley after she confronted her about breaking his heart. "Then again, maybe he won't. I have outgrown this place. Outgrown the town, outgrown the church and outgrown Steve."

Past conversations like this flooded Harley's head as she drove home. She looked at the time. .

It would only be eleven hours until she would be side by side with Steve.

Four hours together with her dream man, the guy that made her heart flutter, that made her blush and stare.

What was she doing to wear?

She ripped open her closet and began rifling through her outfits. Blue? Green? Sexy or demure? What was his favorite color? Did she ever even ask? Maybe she should dress like Shannon used to?

"Don't get your hopes up, girl," she told herself. That voice inside her head that quelled her expectations whenever things were about to get good. But she couldn't help it. Maybe this was God's way of leading them together? At a fund raiser for a missionary trip no less.

Picking out her outfit for tomorrow, Harley started to noodle around on Facebook. She checked out pictures of her, Steve and Shannon hanging out.

Harley stared at the picture of Steve with a long and searching intensity. The photographs brought back memories of his deep voice. The way he smiled and smelled.

She took a slow turn around her room, thinking. Then she knelt down in front of her windowsill and caught her own reflection. Her chestnut brown hair softly back lit, she studied her own face. She was pretty, with big brown eyes, a soft snub tip of a nose and a nice smile.

Harley began to pray aloud, something she hadn't done since grade school. Her voice small and earnest.

She prayed for a chance to win Steve's heart. Just a chance.

CHAPTER TWO

Pastor Owen was nice enough to bring Steve breakfast that morning. He got it from the *Boombrush c*afe where a couple of the parishioners worked.

Steve shoveled the scrambled eggs into his mouth.

"Just wanted to show my appreciation," Owen said. "Plus Harley will be working with you. Figured just in case things got too busy. You know how it is serving this many people."

"Harley is going to work the stand with me?"

"Yeah."

"Oh," Steve said. He knew that the hesitation in his voice did little to disguise the dismay he felt.

Pastor Owen gave him a queer look but didn't pursue any further line of questioning much to Steve's relief. Steve thought that the pastor's personality wavered between being an unfriendly diplomat to warm free spirit.

The church elders didn't know what was up, he thought. They don't keep track of who is dating who or the dynamics involved. They think that just because everyone is involved in the same church that everything is kumbaya. That everyone got along.

"I got the call from Theresa yesterday," Pastor Owen said. "Then Harley happened to be walking by. Perfect kismet. She's great. She works as an accountant now so who better to tally up the sales!"

"Sounds like a plan," Steve said.

"I am sorry things didn't work out with Shannon."

"No worries," Steve replied.

"I know it is none of my business," the pastor continued. "And I'm always there to talk about things of that nature. But remember that things aren't what they appear to be. You may see her on Facebook with some other guy and think 'wow, I am really missing out on her.' But trust me. She's miserable."

"What makes you say that?"

"Trust me," Owen said. "I know women. And these women who go from one guy to the next guy to the next guy have the skin rash of the emotionally insecure. Things don't work out for good reason. Sometimes, we just don't see it."

"Thanks," Steve said, surprised at how forthright the Pastor was. But maybe he knew that not only did Shannon turn her back on him but the church as well.

"Be good, brother," Owen said as he playfully punched Steve on the shoulder and walked off.

"Awkward," Steve mumbled to himself as the pastor walked back inside the church. He thought about what he was going to say to Harley. He had given her the cold shoulder since Shannon had broke up with him. He really didn't know why. Guilt by association, maybe? In hindsight, maybe he should not have done that. But girls stick together even when one of them doesn't treat a member of the opposite sex with Christian kindness.

Thing was that he did find Harley intriguing. The two women were complete opposites in both looks and in the responses that they drew out of Steve. Shannon was attractive in a super model kind of way. Tall, blonde with green eyes and a perfect face. When Steve thought of her, his carnal imagination took over. Her skin tight blouses and the Mediterranean curves of her hips made sure of that.

But there was always that strange sexual antagonism between them. The defining roles that each of them felt obligated to play but didn't really want to. Shannon knew she was a catch. So she liked to test Steve. Cut him deep to see how much it would hurt. And he always kept a stiff upper lip. Until she finally betrayed him.

With Harley, he did not have any sense of hostility at all. Harley was short but cute. Her personality was warm and her voice quiet. He wanted to wrap his arms around her, let her put her face into the crook of his neck. He trusted her in a special way. And imagined her falling sleep in his arms at night like a kitten.

Harley's face had qualities that Shannon's symmetrically perfect face didn't. You could read the sincerity in Harley's eyes. Shannon's smile was small, perfectly polite, and on auto-pilot. Harley's smile was wide and spontaneous. Genuine.

A smile that made Steve's heart flutter.

But it was a heart that did not give itself away easily. And he had to make sure that his attraction for Harley was sincere and not a case of the lonelies.

Out of the corner of his eye, he saw Harley approach. He looked up and smiled.

"Hey now," he said. "Ready to make some people fat today?"

She laughed. "As long as we get fat ourselves. I have been looking forward to trying out the different cookies in between customers."

"I'll start without you," he said as he stuffed one of the cookies in his mouth.

"Steve," she said. "You keep that up and we'll have nothing to sell."

"Yum," he said. "And my name is no longer Steve. It is the Cookie Monster."

"Glad you like it! I made those! White chocolate with oatmeal. Plus a little vanilla for flavor."

"Its really good," he said. "But you're right. I need to stop. If I keep eating it I'll lose my washboard abs."

"Well, we can't have that."

Steve noticed Harley checking out his biceps. Or so he thought. Like so many muscular men he thought that every woman checked him out for his physique.

He held out the chair for Harley to sit down.

"Pastor Owen said you would take care of the money since you're an accountant. And since I'm a big dumb youth minister I'll just sit here and look the part."

"Oh come on," she said, touching his arm. "You're a whole lot more than that!"

She didn't say much but there was something about her demeanor that warmed his heart. He forgot about how much he enjoyed their time together. Forgot about Shannon. Harley was her own person.

And Steve become very interested in learning more about her.

CHAPTER 3

Harley was having a hard time concentrating when Steve stood so close to her. She constantly monitored him out of the corner of her eye and tried to gauge if his response to her was favorable. They had not been in such close proximity together in a long time. In fact, she never recalled a time when they were alone together without Shannon.

She liked Steve's easy manner as he greeted the parishioners as they dallied about. The church went all out for July 4th and it was the place to be. The music was in full force, there was barbecue, the bake sale, different contests and games. At night, they would enjoy the fireworks because they were so close to the Oakland Coliseum which hosted the area's show.

Harley took extra time to make her cupcakes and cookies stand out from the rest. On occasions like church bake sales she took the extra time to show off her pastry skills to the congregation...and to Steve. She may not be as beautiful as Shannon but she was much better in the kitchen. That had to count for something, she laughed to herself.

Christine, a middle-aged woman with four kids, waltzed up to their sales table. Everyone called her "Pookie Chips" for reasons that Harley never understood. She wore a dress or moo-moo that looked more like a shower curtain, complete with pictures of ducks and fish. This was kept in place by a string that went around her ample waist and her hair was still in curlers.

"Hi all!" she squawked in a voice that made Harley wince.

"Hello," Steve and Harley answered in unison.

Her kids stared in silence at the baked goods.

"Those look irresistible," Christine pointed at the cupcakes but eyeballed Steve up and down, her face alight with flirty intentions.

Jesus, what would your husband think woman, Harley thought as she could see the lustful train of thought in Christine's eyes. Then again, she could not resist the impure thoughts of her own.

"How many would you like?" Steve asked.

"None for me," Christine said. "I'm watching my figure. But how about one each for the boys?"

One of the kids took one of the cookies and began gnawing at it like it was a piece of beef jerky. Then he spat it out.

"Chad!" Christine yelled. "Where are your manners?"

"Pah!" the boy said. "Yuck!"

Why you little turd, Harley thought, narrowing her eyes at the boy for a brief moment.

"How about some cupcakes instead?" Steve offered.

Harley liked how Steve remained unaffected and easy going. Harley imagined them growing old and gray together. Steve as an elderly grandfather handing out hot dogs to their noisy grandchildren while she came into a garden with hot cookies for them.

Ah, but who was she kidding. Things never worked out for her. If anything he would be married to some fashion model or former cheerleader sharing an aperitif in Paris. She would be stuck here, in the same church, waiting for some dream man that would never show up.

"Nice kids," Steve said as they walked away.

Harley smirked. "Sure."

"You ever thought about it?"

"What?"

"Having kids?"

"Oh, sure, of course."

Steve nodded his head slightly. "That's actually rare. I mean, I see a lot of women nowadays that don't really seem to want any. One of my cousins on posted on Facebook that she didn't want to have children. Ever. Then a couple of my other female cousins chimed in agreeing with her along with her friends. It become a huge long post of women posting that they didn't want any. None of them posted the reasons why though."

"It's tough, of course," Harley said slowly, looking to find words that would make her sound thoughtful. "And scary. I agree that you get a lot of insight on people from their Facebook page."

"Are we friends?"

"Huh?"

"On Facebook?"

"Oh, no. I don't think so."

"I'll add you later. Kinda funny that we never added each other since we were both friends with Shannon."

"Yeah," Harley said. "I'm not a really Facebook person." Yeah, right, she thought.

Steve turned his attention back to an approaching customer.

Why did he ask about her attitudes about children? Harley thought with a delayed reaction. Was he interested and gauging her response to see if they aligned with his own. Harley had a bad habit of taking mundane conversations and extrapolating them into different tangents. Why? What if? What?

A bad habit she could not break. She couldn't help herself. She loved his pleasant demeanor, deep voice and long eyelashes. But what would a man like him see in her?

The self-talk began in Harley's head. That voice that reared its ugly head whenever she tried something new or wanted something that she considered out of her reach for whatever reason.

Harley inherited low self-esteem from her mother. Her mom was "only a housewife" as described by her father. Her father ascended to become a fire captain but routinely abused her mother with vicious put-downs. He destroyed her personality.

But for Harley's religious faith, she would have gone down the same road as her mother who was trapped in a manic depressive cycle. Harley only talked to her when she was on "happy time" as she called it when she was a kid. And her Mom did go to church occasionally and profess the faith. She could be outgoing for a little while then become agitated and withdrawn without warning. The inexplicable worthlessness that infected her personality would never go away.

Harley wondered often if she inherited her mom's personality. That maybe, with God's help she could be different.

"Are you okay?" Steve asked.

"Of course," Harley said. "Why?"

"You look like you went someplace else there for a minute," Steve laughed, taking out his Smartphone. "Let's see, I'll add you now."

Harley looked over and could see him logging in to Facebook.

Little did he know that she had browsed through his pages the night before. She wanted to see if he were dating anyone. But he had very little on his page and remained a mystery.

A mystery that she had to figure out on her own.

CHAPTER 4

Get me out of here, Steve thought. He knew the set up would be awkward with Harley but he didn't know it would be this awkward.

Now that he thought about it, he felt as if he were being set up. People in the church just loved playing matchmaker. Everyone knew about his break-up with Shannon and old Pastor Owens may be trying to play cupid. Easy for them to do. Why the hell do they always think that people in the church need to hook up with one another?

Luckily, the church festival did get busy and the parishioners kept Harley and Steve busy. Steve never collected so much money in his life. After a few hours, people started to file out and say good bye.

His day from hell was almost over.

"You finally look happy to be here. Or happy you're leaving," Harley said.

"Well, we did a good job. Look, only one cupcake left."

"I know this must have been awkward for you," Harley said. "Being with me."

Whoa. Steve appreciated Harley's honesty.

"No," he said. "Why would you say that?"

"Because of my connection to Shannon. We, you know, used to be friends and now we don't hang out anymore."

"Things happen," Steve said. "Things change. People change. No reason why we can't get along."

"I wish things were different. I mean, I wish things could just work out the way they are supposed to."

"And how are they supposed to?" Steve asked, holding back a laugh but really interested in what she had to say.

"Without people getting hurt."

"I'm not hurt," Steve said.

Harley shook her head as if to say it is okay to not talk about it.

Then he realized that she was probably talking about herself. The cold shoulder that he had given her was wrong. She had nothing to do with Shannon's behavior and he should not have automatically assumed that she had taken her side. He had given her the cold shoulder because he liked having the power over her.

Not talking to her. Ignoring her. It was all about power.

Steve felt ashamed. He knew he had been wrong.

"I was thinking maybe we can get some sushi after?" he offered. "I remember that was your favorite. Kappa maki, right?"

Was this a good idea? Did he really want to go through this all over again? Date a girl from the church and have the whole thing blow up in his face again?

Harley's eyes grew big. As if she were about to collapse from shock.

"You okay?" he asked.

"No," she said. "I'm fine. You really want to have lunch with me?"

"Well," he said. "Yeah. Can you come?"

"Yeah," she said. "Like I would turn down sushi."

"Okay."

What were they going to talk about? He racked his brain for reasons why he was doing this.

The comfort zone. He thought to himself. He promised himself that he would get out of his comfort zone and stop doing only the things that he felt comfortable doing. He had to make amends with Harley somehow. Had to stop pouting around mentally because things didn't work out with Shannon and get out.

Steve had his own private conversations with God in his head. He thought maybe all that his grandmother and mother instilled in him were true as they taught him that God always leads us to the right person.

Steve wanted a clean slate, to forget about Shannon. But he had so much anger and shame over the break up. So many expectations that were unfulfilled.

It was the way Shannon led him on. She had him believing that she was a Christian woman at heart. That she really loved him. But at the end of the day it was all a lie. Were all women like that? Would they all jump ship the moment a better deal comes along?

He looked at Harley. Her genuine smile and bright eyes bespoke of someone who would always be true. But he saw the same qualities in Shannon once. He told himself the same lies. *She's different. She wouldn't hurt me.*

Mark and Channing, two twin brothers, came up to their table.

"Ready to close up shop?" they asked. Collecting the money box, they were part of the clean up crew and were eager to get started.

"Ready to go?" Steve asked Harley.

Her smile gave him her answer.

CHAPTER 6

Is this really happening? Did Steve really ask her to lunch? Harley had to pinch herself to make sure she wasn't dreaming. She felt like laughing with joy. A nervous giggle that she did whenever she felt happy.

What next, she thought? Would they hold hands? She didn't try to push her luck. But what if this was only a platonic date?

Shut up! She told the voice in her head that always brought her down.

He held the door open for her as they reached his Ford Explorer. Harley reached over and opened unlocked the driver side door for him.

"Thanks so much for this," Harley said as he got in.

"Of course," he said with a smile. "Thanks for lifting up the button. Not many girls do that anymore."

She smiled. He started the car and they were off. It was really happening!

"Why me?"

"Huh?"

"We haven't talked all that much recently. I thought-well, I didn't think we'd every talk again let alone have lunch. Why the change of heart?"

"No change of heart," Steve lied. "I've just been busy. And you've been busy."

"I'm at the church every Sunday."

"Yeah, but at church everyone is watching. Everyone talks. All it takes is for us to be in the hallway, alone, having an innocent conversation and the next thing you know people will be handing us cards for wedding planners."

"Yeah, people talk too much."

Steve shrugged his shoulders as if to say 'what can you do'.

"We can't even be friends. Have a perfectly platonic relationship without people talking. Kinda ridiculous if you ask me."

"Yeah," Harley said, her voice soft. Great, she thought, he just wants to be friends.

They arrived at the mini-mall where the Sushi Palace was. The "palace" stood in between a dry cleaners and a coffee shop.

Harley walked close to Steve and saw her reflection in the front glass window of the restaurant. Wow, she thought, we do look good together. She wanted to pursue that "friendship" conversation a bit further but was afraid she would confirm would she already knew. That he was not doing this because of romantic intentions.

The topic of Shannon had not reared its ugly head yet. She expected him to ask how she was doing or what not. Not that she would know. But she did wonder what would Shannon say at a time like this.

Only three other couples were in the restaurant. They were seated next to a mother and her teenage son.

The waiter handed them their menus and Harley could not help but overhear the conversation next to them.

"Get ready to get divorced," the mother said to her son. "Relationships just don't last. Sometimes it takes two or three times to get it right and even then you still may not be happy."

"But statistics show that second and third marriages end in divorce at a higher rate than first marriages."

"Don't tell me the numbers," the mother continued. "Relationships don't last. I am just trying to prepare you. Don't get your hopes up."

Harley returned her attention to the menu.

"Let's see, what's good here?" Steve said idly scanning over his own menu and giving Harley a quick smile.

"Everything sounds good," Harley said, licking her lips. She loved Japanese food. Sharing her favorite ethnic food with the man of her dreams. What more could she ask for?

"Thanks so much for this," she said.

"Wow," he said. "Of course."

"Can I get you folks anything to start?" the waiter, a thin teenaged boy asked in a squeaky voice.

Yeah, Harley wanted to say. If you're a genie give me about fifty years of love and romance with the man sitting across from me.

"I'll take the cucumber roll," she said instead.

"I want what she wants," Steve said.

Harley smiled to herself. If you only knew, Steve. If you only knew.

CHAPTER 6

The food arrived and it looked delicious. To Harley at least. Steve still had not gotten used to the idea of eating raw fish. A cheeseburger and fries kind of guy, he opted for the Teriyaki beef as his main course.

"I love this time of year," Harley said in between bites. "Most people love Christmas the most. But I love the Fourth of July."

"I love holidays, period," Steve chuckled. "But since I'm so low on seniority at the hospital I usually don't get the days off."

"That's right," Harley said. "Jesus, I don't know how you do it. Working as an RN and then doubling down as a Youth Minister."

"The ministry is just a way of giving back. It can't support me. I don't think I'll go into it full time like become a pastor or anything. It is tempting though because working in the emergency room is stressful."

"I can't imagine."

"But I can't complain. I was just drawn to it for whatever reason. People say they have a calling in life. For me, it is whatever you have a passion for. Whatever you have a passion for then that is what you have to do."

"That's what I'm struggling with. I don't have a passion for numbers, per se. I mean no one dreams about assets and liabilities when they're a kid."

"But you went to cooking school right?"

"Pastry chef," she said. "Again, it is not really a calling. Just something I enjoy doing."

"Then that is what you should do."

Harley shrugged her shoulders.

"Sorry, I shouldn't be giving you advice. I mean, who am I?"

"No worries," she said. "I like these kind of conversations. I mean, everyone talks about what they do but no one talks about why they do it. I mean, I would like to help out at the hospital. But I didn't go into the medical field. Didn't have the calling."

"You can volunteer," Steve said. "We have people helping out in the emergency room. Some of it is the little things like keeping the linen fresh. Warming blankets. Transporting patients."

"I see."

"But a lot of volunteers stop in the rooms of patients and just talk to them. You know, sometimes that is really all it takes. These old people are lonely. And I think a lot of them just want that interaction, you know? There aren't enough people out there who really care. Not enough Christians who put their faith into practice."

"I can see myself doing that," Harley offered. "I mean, volunteering at the hospital. That's been something I have been wanting to do for awhile now. Putting myself out there and helping people. Not sure if I can do much though."

"I'll send you the link to sign up, seeing we're Facebook friends now."

"Sounds like a plan."

Steve decided to not let Harley in on the fact that she would be "shadowing" him during this volunteer training. His supervisor invariably allowed new volunteers to follow Steve around the department for a few days as they become acquainted in the emergency room. But here he was thinking of ways to avoid and ignore Harley and now he was inviting her to be a part of his work life! What was wrong with him.

"How is your mom doing?"

He had to change the subject.

"Better I suppose," Harley sighed. "Every day without an incident is a good day so I have to be grateful for that."

"I see."

"I impressed that you haven't asked about Shannon at all."

"Who?"

"Haha," Harley said. "Okay, be that way."

"Okay, fine," he said. "How is she?"

Harley shook her head. "I don't think she's happy."

"Really?" Steve asked. "I saw her picture profile on Facebook and she's giving this guy a huge kiss."

"Stay off Facebook," she said. "And looks are always deceiving. Be content in knowing that she made a mistake and she's paying for it."

"Well, there is no going back to me."

"She puts on a false front and says she's happy that she is over you. But I don't buy it."

"I've moved on," Steve said. "She's in the past. I don't even think about her."

"I don't buy that either."

CHAPTER 7

Aaargh. Harley, what have you done aside from showing the dexterity to put both feet in your mouth? Steve sat there with a poker face but she knew that her snarky remark had put him on edge.

She had to learn to speak the truth in love. And sometimes that meant saying nothing at all.

But she told the truth. But so what? She had no right to bring up his personal life. Steve had been a perfect gentleman and expressed no desire to discuss his love life.

"I apologize," Harley said. "That was wrong. Who am I to say that?"

"No worries," Steve said. "Experiencing the loss of a relationship takes time. Sometimes we do have to lie to ourselves in order to make pain go away."

"I'm sorry," she repeated. Harley felt like crying. She ruined a perfectly good day. She spent hours with Steve and was coming off as a busybody during lunch.

"It is good to talk about her," Steve said. "I don't think we'll have much of a friendship if we avoid the subject. She was part of my life. She's your best friend. So it is really silly just to avoid talking about her."

"You're right."

"I mean I still have people at work that ask me about that 'hot chick' I am dating. There's this guy named Dale that works in security. Shannon came down to have lunch with me one day and the guys eyes just bugged out. Said I was a damn lucky guy and was nice to me ever since. Even guys treat you differently when you're dating a quote unquote hot chick."

"Women do too. I mean they'll look at you and think, hmm, there must be something about that guy."

"Whatever," Steve said. "But like you said, appearances are never ever what they appear."

Harley shook her head. "Nope. Never. But I have to confess something. "

"What's that?"

"I told her off."

"Who?"

"Shannon."

"I told her what a great mistake she was making. That if she let you go, she was making the biggest mistake of her life. This guy that she is dating is not even a Christian. Not like that should be the ultimate measuring stick for a good person but he really has nothing in common with her background. You on the other hand are-"

"What?"

Harley wanted to say 'perfect.'

"A great guy."

"Thanks," Steve laughed. "Sounds like I have someone in my corner."

"Oh we went at it, believe me," Harley said. "Ultimately, it is her life. But you were my friend too. I didn't like seeing you hurt."

"Thanks," he said. "I didn't know you felt that way."

"There are a lot of things you don't know about me, Mister Steve."

"Well, I will do my research," he laughed as he held up his cup of tea. "Cheers! To loyal friends who stick up for you."

"Cheers to that," Harley said.

CHAPTER 8

Steve didn't know where this was going. He felt sorry for Harley in a way. She had hung out with Shannon all of her life and always seem to have been a second fiddle. She played the role of the good Christian girl to Shannon who looked the part. There had to have been a point in her life when she said "Marcia, Marcia, Marcia" like Jan Brady.

"It was fun hanging out together," Steve said. "Although a part of me thinks that sometimes Shannon had you come along because she didn't know what to say."

"Her security blanket," Harley said "I didn't have a boyfriend. And I think she waned me to feel a part of things. She wasn't all bad."

"Yeah."

"But we shouldn't talk about her in the past tense like she's dead."

Steve laughed. "Remember the time when we went to that concert in Santa Cruz? And she got all mad because we weren't rocking out with her. "

"Well, that band that was playing was horrible. Horrible. I know that sounds mean."

"No, they were bad. I remember there was a man walking by holding his fingers to his ears."

"I think the funnest time we had was when we went to the zoo. Do you remember?"

"Yeah," Steve said. "When the monkey got pissed and started throwing his bananas at us."

"Yeah, what was up with that?"

"And it hit me square in the face!"

"Why did it hit you? I mean I should have been chivalrous and stepped in front of you!"

"Yeah, thanks for nothing."

"I miss those times," Steve said.

"Me too."

"Just hanging out, you know? My Dad always warned me against having that kind of philosophy."

"How so?"

"He didn't want me to be a layabout, partying all the time. There were so many people in his family that were drunks. He used to say 'you don't want to sit around all day and scratch your ass.'"

"Ha, ha, your Dad used to say that? He seemed so polite."

"Your only seeing one side of him. He used to say 'you don't want to sit around, belching an farting in a bar someplace. Go out and make something of yourself.' But you know what? Sometimes I just want to do nothing. Sit under stars and talk. Lay in the grass. And just chill out. Whatever chill out means. I like the sound of the word."

"I know," she said. "I mean how did we ever get to the point where we are working jobs that we hate. Dating people we don't really like and then coming to the point where it is like you know, there has to be something more than this. There has to be something more."

Steve nodded his head.

"Sometimes I think if I just found the right girl, everything would be okay. The job wouldn't be so tough. Life wouldn't be so tough."

"I pray for you a lot," Harley said.

"Really?"

"Like whenever they talk about something happening like a fire or a shooting I know that you might be dealing with it at the hospital in some way. Or when they were talking about the Ebola virus. I worried about you. Was afraid that somehow, someway you would be exposed to it."

"No worries here," Steve said chuckling. "But it is nice to know that someone was out there thinking about me."

"We should be going," she said.

Steve was tempted to say 'so soon.' He had not expected to have enjoyed her company so thoroughly. And he didn't realize how much he was in her thoughts.

Because now she was in his.

CHAPTER 9

Steve had dropped her off at the cafe near her apartment because she wanted to get some coffee. He walked around and opened the door for her. They said their goodbyes and then he hugged her.

Everyone hugs nowadays, she thought. Even men exchange "bro hugs."

But still, she had to read something into their hug. He felt him press himself against her body for that one brief microsecond and then release. She wished that moment could have lasted forever.

Harley couldn't look him in the eyes after that. She felt her whole face flush red and had to walk away.

It was a platonic thing, she kept repeating to herself. But maybe that was the pessimist inside her bringing her down again. She didn't look at his face after so she could not gauge his reaction.

She had prayed for that moment. Prayed that one day they would be on speaking terms again and in one magic day all of her prayers had been answered. She closed her eyes and whispered a "thank you, Lord."

And when she opened her yes and looked out the window of the cafe, she saw that an old woman fall flat on her face.

Harley raced outside and helped the woman up.

"Are you okay?"

"Oh, I think so," the woman said. She looked to be in her eighties and wore a tweed overcoat.

Harley looked down and saw one of her slippers caught in a crack in the pavement. She knelt down and slipped it back on the woman's bare foot.

"God bless you," the woman said.

"Are you sure you're okay?" she asked.

The woman nodded her head. "I'll be all right."

"Just a little scratched up is all," Harley said.

"God bless you," the old woman said as she walked away.

'I wish' she thought to herself as she made her way to her apartment. She looked back at the old woman to make sure she would make it across the street okay and then continued on.

Just once, she thought. Just once if things could work out between her and Steve. But after all of the rude questions she had asked she wasn't sure he would want to go through that again.

CHAPTER 10

Steve stood in the emergency room parking lot and looked at the fireworks going off.

He thought about the fireworks show last year when he sat on the blanket with Shannon and watched the night sky.

Oh, how appearances can deceive! He remembered the selfie they took of each other as the fireworks went off in behind them. Then they kissed, took the selfie and posted it on Facebook.

"Fireworks!" people wrote in the comment box underneath.

Truth be told,he had a great time that night. Just sitting and talking with Shannon. But in hindsight that was the beginning of the end.

He remembered how quiet she was that night. She was already plotting out her exit plan.

"How do you like it?" Steve remembered saying, pointing up to the show.

'It's okay," she would say flatly.

Little did he know she had already been seeing the lawyer. Her boss at the firm where she was working.

He remembered driving her home that evening. Kissing her goodnight and wondering where there relationship was going. It was one of those flat goodbyes where he knew something was wrong but couldn't pinpoint what the problem was.

Steve couldn't help but imagine what it would be like to watch the fireworks with Harley. She would get into it. Probably lean into him and hug him for safety whenever a big explosion would go off.

Shannon would never do something like that. Everything had a 'been there, done that' feeling with her.

Steve had made up his mind. He would ask Harley out. Who cares if it was awkward? They would find out if there were made for each other. That's why people date!

He walked back in through the emergency room and saw all of the nurses with in hands up, don't shoot posture.

"Just give me what I want!" the man said. He had a crazed look in his eye, food particles in his beard and a handgun pointed at the nurse's station.

"You there," the man said, spotting Steve. "Put your hands where I can see them."

Steve immediately put up his hands.

"Easy now," he said. "What is it that you want?"

"What I have been saying!"

"I can help you," Steve he felt his voice crack with nervousness. "I am the one that can help."

"The doc was supposed to fill my pain meds!" he said. "Y'all are treating me like I'm some kind of criminal. A Criminal! I'm in pain!

"Steve!" one of the nurses shouted.

"Take it easy," Steve said.

"Take it easy, my ass!" The man waved his gun around. "Everyone against the wall. Everyone!"

"Sir," Steve said. "We have other patients. We have to care for the patients."

"I don't care!" the man said. "I want my meds!"

He pointed the gun directly at Steve.

"I'll kill you!" he said. "I'll kill you if I have to!"

Steve looked at the end of the man's gun. His life flashed before his eyes. He thought about his mom and brother. And then he thought about Harley. The possibility of never seeing her again. The life they would never have.

CHAPTER 11

Harley could hear the fireworks going off outside her apartment building. Some of the explosions came from the Oakland Coliseum. The others came from the neighborhood kids setting off "jumping jacks", small firecrackers that exploded like popcorn.

She looked out her window and could see the hospital in bright lights. She thought about Steve and what kind of tasks he would be doing at the moment.

Her cell phone rang. Could it be him?

The caller ID showed Theresa's number.

"Hey, Tee," Harley said.

"Hey girl," Mags said. "Just wanted to thank you for taking over with the sales."

"No problem. It was fun actually."

"I heard."

"What's that supposed to mean?"

"That you and Steve were quite a team."

"Oh really-"

"And that you went to lunch together," Theresa said in a teasing voice.

"Jesus, does everyone in that church talk? I suppose you know what we ordered."

"I think you both had a large helping of cupid's arrow."

"Haha, yeah, I wish."

"Just go for it," Theresa said. "If it doesn't work out, it doesn't work out."

"He's got a broken heart," Harley said. "He really loved Shannon. And I'm cool with that. It shows a capacity to love. But I don't think I can ever replace her in his heart."

"But that's over with-"

"I can the hurt in his eyes. He still thinks about her, despite what he says. It is something that is really hard to overcome Words alone aren't going to mend his heart I know that. I just-"

"Keep trying, girl-wait hold on."

Harley didn't know why she was opening up to Theresa. She had to talk to someone. She couldn't talk to Shannon about her boy troubles obviously but Theresa seemed safe.

"Oh my God, Harley, is Steve in the emergency room?"

"Yeah, why?"

"There's some kind of hostage situation going on there. A gunman!"

"Oh my God!"

Harley rushed to turn on her television and saw nothing on the news. Then she sprinted over to her PC and googled it.

Sure enough, the headline read "hostage situation in hospital."

Steve, Harley thought. Just please let Steve be okay.

CHAPTER 12

"You don't want to do this, sir." Steve said. He now talked with a calmness and peace he didn't expect. He said a silent prayer, asking God for help. Then, almost like magic, he felt a sense of composure and assurance.

"See?" the gunman railed. "Why does it take someone to have a gun before people talk them to with respect! To be treated like a human being! It takes a gun!"

"People forget sometimes," Steve shook his head. "They forget that their talking to a man. They forget that they're talking to a person with feelings and a heart. We get busy and we forget. We're human too. We're sorry. I'm sorry that you felt the need to get a gun. It should have never have come to that."

"I just want my meds," the man said, his voice now lowered an octave. Someone had heard him and he no longer felt the need to threaten violence.

"Put the gun down, brother," Steve said softly. "Okay? Put the gun down."

"You all made me do this! I didn't want to do this! No one listens! Do you hear me? No one listens!"

The man dropped to his knees and began to cry.

Steve approached with caution, his hands in the hair. Then he knelt down aside the man.

"I know it's hard It's frustrating. We think no one sees us. We think that everyone is ignoring us. That no one listens."

"My wife died," the man whispered. "My wife died two months ago. She had a bad heart. We both had bad hearts. I just thought I would go before her. I can't-"

Steve put his hand on the man's shoulder. He waited several minutes before he spoke as the man looked like he was going to say something but couldn't. Years of suppressed emotions could not be articulated because he didn't know how.

"I'm sorry, brother."

"I don't know what to do," the man said.

"I'm sorry," the man started to sob, his chest heaving with every tear.

Steve reached over and gently pried the gun away from the man's hand.

"We just need to talk, okay? Just relax and talk."

The man nodded his head.

With that the SWAT team burst through the door.

"Put your hands up!"

The man bolted up, his eyes like a deer caught in the headlights.

Five men slammed him to the ground. They spun him around like a rag doll and handcuffed him.

Steve wanted to intervene somehow, chastise the cops to go easy on the guy. But no one would listen. Just like the man said.

No one listens.

"Everyone okay?" Steve asked the staff, getting back into charge nurse mode. The staff moved to hug each other, the traumatic moment now gone out of their lives. "Room A needs that EKG. Let's re-check the labs on everyone."

Steve knew that the sooner they got back to normalcy the sooner they would forget what happened. Life would go on. No matter how petty or severe the problem, things moved on.

He wondered about the man and his mother.

A hour or so later, a hospital representative came and wanted Steve to address the media.

"You've got to be kidding?" he asked as she whisked him outside to greet throng of reporters. A yellow tape had been stretched across the hospital parking lot as people from the community had arrived in droves. They saw the situation unfold on the news and wanted to come first hand to get a look as if it were a show.

But in the crowd he saw Harley. He made a bee-line toward her and they hugged.

A hug that lasted more than a few seconds.

"I just had to see if you were okay?" she whispered.

"Yeah," Steve said. "I'm fine. Everyone is a little shaken up is all." He wanted her to stay and talk and maybe have cup of coffee with him in the cafeteria.

"Steve!" the hospital representative called out.

"You have to go, I know," Harley said

"No, I don't," he said.

Then he kissed her on the lips.

Harley could not breath for a moment. They stopped kissing and she had to catch her breath.

"What," she said finally. "Does this mean?"

"It means, I don't want to ever lose you."

Harley hugged him hard.

She felt a pounding in her chest. Her heart beat so fast that it warmed her entire body.

Nothing ever felt so right.

www.ingramcontent.com/pod-product-compliance
Lightning Source LLC
Chambersburg PA
CBHW061453150726
47987CB00001B/430